DAMAGE

ANYA PARRISH

DAMAGE

Woodbury, Minnesota

First Edition
First Printing, 2011

Cover design by Ellen Lawson
Cover image of claw scratches © iStockphoto.com/Piai
          background © iStockphoto.com/Emre Yildiz
          girl © PhotoAlto

Flux, an imprint of Llewellyn Worldwide Ltd.

Library of Congress Cataloging-in-Publication Data
Parrish, Anya
  Damage / Anya Parrish.—1st ed.
    p. cm.
  Summary: After their bus crashes while on a school field trip, fifteen-year-old Dani and seventeen-year-old Jesse discover that for years they have both been stalked by unexplainable and evil beings trying to harm them, and their further investigations reveal the depth of the horrors they continue to experience.
  ISBN 978-0-7387-2700-4
  [1. Horror stories. 2. Violence—Fiction. 3. Experiments—Fiction. 4. Love—Fiction.] I. Title.
  PZ7.P2451Dam 2011
  [Fic]—dc23

                    2011014157

Flux
Llewellyn Worldwide Ltd.
2143 Wooddale Drive
Woodbury, MN 55125-2989
www.fluxnow.com

Printed in the United States of America

Acknowledgments

Many, many heartfelt thanks to the publishing team at Flux. You are what writer dreams are made of! Thanks also to Jessica Verday and Caitlin Kittredge, two generous, talented ladies who helped make my year. Special thanks to my husband and two little boys, who are the reason and the everything and so much damned fun. More special thanks to readers of this book. I appreciate you so very much.

For the survivors

prologue

There was a time when I prayed for Rachel to be real.

During those long nights alone at the hospital, when Mom and Dad left to fight in the privacy of our own home, when all I could feel was pain and sleep lingered just out of reach—the string on a balloon bouncing against the ceiling—I wished and wished and *prayed* for Rachel to be a real girl.

I would hold very still, focusing with everything in me until I could make out her dress and the back of her shining brown hair, until I could see those mischievous blue eyes peeking at me over her shoulder. I knew she was smiling, though I never saw her face.

Her eyes told me she was smiling. They made promises I knew she would keep. They promised fun and laughter and escape from a world of sharp needles and food that tasted of rubbing alcohol and burnt marshmallows. For a year everything had tasted charred, ruined. Dad said it was a side effect of the medicine they were using to make me better. He said ice cream would taste good again once I was well.

Once I was well, they would lower my dosage and I would see how wonderful everything tasted, how wonderful everything smelled, how wonderful it would be to eat and run and play and be the healthy child I had never been.

Once I was well, I would see.

But I wasn't well.

The fluttering near my heart—birds trapped in a cage of bone—was fading, but it seemed to be taking forever. I was eight years old. A month was forever. A year was an eternity. I had been trapped for an eternity in that bed with the scratchy sheets, in that room with the cold floor I could feel even through my slippers and the night nurse who smelled so strongly of coffee it seemed she'd bathed in it.

I wanted out. I wanted a way to forget. Rachel gave me both.

I'd followed her out of my room before, trailing her to adventure in the closed cafeteria or up to the roof where we'd danced under the stars, but that night was different. The smelly nurse was right there at her desk when Rachel slipped from my room. She'd always waited until the nurse went to refill her cup before beckoning me out into the hall. Not this time. Now, she walked straight up to the desk, grabbed the nurse's cup, and threw it.

Hot liquid splattered over cold tile. The stale hospital air bloomed with a sharp, bitter smell. The nurse cried out and turned to clean up the mess and I nearly fainted.

That coffee cup had confirmed it. My mother was wrong. Rachel wasn't an imaginary friend. Rachel was *real*. I watched her knock a chart from the desk in awe, more excited than I could remember.

Christmas morning had nothing on Rachel.

Come on, silly. I heard her voice in my head, louder than before.

Her blue eyes flashed above her shoulder before she turned and ran. I followed, creeping past the still bent-over nurse and chasing after Rachel. My heart thudded dully in my ears; my lungs struggled to draw breaths deeper than I was accustomed to. I wasn't as strong as Rachel, but I was getting stronger. The medicine was working. For the first time, I believed my father's promise. I was going to be well. I was going to grow up to be tall and strong and put the miserable days of my childhood behind me.

And Rachel would be there with me, a real friend only I could see, a piece of magic only I could touch.

I trailed her laughter and the soft tapping of her dress shoes down one hallway and then another, past rooms that smelled of disease and pain, past the muffled sounds of a sleepless kid watching *SpongeBob SquarePants* after hours, past the beeping of machines and the buzzing of florescent lights and the endless concrete walls with their cheery murals painted by kids who were long dead.

There were ghosts on the ninth floor of Baptist Memorial, the place where kids went to die, but Rachel wasn't one of them. I was more sure of that than ever.

Come on, we're nearly there. I could hear the excitement

in her voice and hurried up the stairs marked *No Exit*, the ones that led to the roof and the stars. The hospital was set far back from the road, surrounded by thick pine trees that taunted the sick kids inside with their greenness. On a clear night, there were always stars.

I wondered if we were going to dance tonight? I wondered if this time I would be able to hear the music that Rachel heard? She'd said the stars could sing and someday I would hear them.

I wanted to hear them. So badly.

I hurried up the winding staircase, out of breath and tasting salt on my tongue by the time I reached the top and threw open the door. I was suddenly terribly thirsty, but I ignored the scratchiness in my mouth. Not a smart thing to do when you have diabetes, but I didn't care. I didn't want to think about being sick. Rachel was real, the world wasn't the same dull, hopeless place anymore. It was something more, something enchanted.

The ash gray of the roof shimmered before me in the moonlight, a road littered with diamonds, a field full of fireflies where Rachel and I could play unobserved. I saw her standing on the opposite side of the great expanse. For once, she faced me directly instead of peeking over her shoulder. Her hair hung in shining waves over her face, shadowing her features, but I knew I would be able to see her if I got closer.

I couldn't wait to see her. I wanted to watch her smile, I wanted to laugh and throw my slender arms around her neck and spin. I'd never had a best friend before. I wanted to thank Rachel for coming to me, for choosing me out of all the sick little girls in the world.

I ran, jumping over rough patches in the roof, light and full of joy. I knew the end was coming. Soon I would be out of the hospital forever, soon I would be free of tests and medicines and pains in the night.

Maybe sooner than you think. She lifted her face.

The moonlight was a hand catching her under the chin, holding her in place, forcing me to look long and hard and see her for what she really was.

"Rachel," I gasped, a part of me thinking that speaking her name would fix things.

It didn't.

Rachel was broken. Where her mouth should have been there was only a thin, red line, a wound that gaped and bled when she smiled. Rachel wasn't real, after all. And she wasn't my friend.

By the time I saw the broken place in the wall surrounding the roof, the one Rachel had been blocking with her slim body, I was flying through it. I twisted in the air, breath catching and holding as I watched myself as if from a distance. I could see the terror on my own face, watch my arms and legs churn through the air against a background of utter blackness.

There were no stars. They were hidden behind the clouds, unwilling to be witnesses to my murder.

She had always planned to kill me. I felt that truth in the eager fingers she used to pry my hands away from the stone I'd been lucky enough to latch on to. She shook with excitement as her nails bit into my flesh. I clung and screamed, long and hard and loud, the sound a celebration of my newfound health. I would never have been able to scream like that before.

I believe that scream saved my life. That scream made a woman two floors down open her window and look out, and up, just in time. Even though she was sick—cancer that later killed her—she reached for me. And when her arms closed around my waist, she didn't let go, even when the momentum of my fall nearly pulled her out the window.

The newspaper called it a miracle. My mother called it attempted suicide. My father called it a horrible side effect of an overdose of experimental medication. My doctors altered my treatment, my mother brought in a shrink, and I learned to say that Rachel was a product of my own imagination who didn't come around anymore.

I lied.

For days, weeks—a second eternity of lying awake in my bed praying I wouldn't hear her shoes tapping down the hallway—I lied. But she always came.

At first with friendly, dancing eyes, trying to lure me in as she'd done before, and then with knives she'd stolen from the cafeteria and syringes of fluid she tried to slip into my IV. She devoted her imaginary existence to my death, and with each attempt she got closer and closer to killing me. I lived in fear that, sooner or later, she would catch me unaware and our terrifying game would be done.

Then one day, she was just…gone.

By the time Rachel stopped coming to visit, I weighed

less than the five-year-old girl down the hall. I looked like a monster, a haunted thing that prowled the children's floor of the hospital with sunken eyes and fingers that worried at the scabs on my skin until they bled.

It took months for me to trust that Rachel was really gone, years to convince myself I'd just been a sick, crazy kid with an overactive imagination. But I finally did it. I pulled it together, I got well, I got out of the hospital and I never looked back.

On the day before the crash I was a determinedly average kid. I got A's and B's and the occasional C, I was obsessed with becoming a professional dancer, I wrote angry things about my stepmother in my journal, and dreamed of the day I'd be free to be all the things I was going to be.

I didn't dream of death, but it seemed death had been dreaming of me.

One

Dani

The bus smells of diesel, old sandwiches, the ghosts of sweaty soccer players, and opportunity. Sweet, shiny opportunity.

I suck in a deep breath and almost smile, but don't. Even on a day like this one, with the winter sun shining through the smeary bus windows and an entire twelve hours of freedom and New York City exploration spreading out before me like brightly colored beads on a wire, there's no reason to let my guard down.

I don't smile when people are watching. I don't frown, either. I strive for neutrality and balance.

Every winter morning, I pull on khaki pants, a white collared shirt, and a navy sweater. Every day, I brush my long, reddish-brown hair into a low ponytail and sweep on mascara and a touch of lip gloss. I look tidy and pretty enough not to be teased, plain and unassuming enough not to be threatening.

Pleasant. Invisible. Just the way I like it.

"So did you give your stepmom the note?" Mina asks. I don't miss the predatory excitement in her voice.

Mina is rarely pleasant, and never invisible.

Today, she wears her blue-and-white-plaid uniform skirt rolled up at the waist to show off more of her strong, dancer's legs, paired with scarred, black motorcycle boots. Her chin-length black hair is flat-ironed into aggressive points and her eyeliner is thick and hostile.

If she weren't five inches shorter than my five eight, I would never have been brave enough to say "hello" to her on her first day of ballet class two years ago. Mina was even scarier then, before she brought up her grades enough to get into Madisonville Prep and was forced to remove her numerous piercings and adhere to the private school dress code.

"Was she crushed that you don't think of her as your BFF?" Mina asks, in a perfect imitation of my stepmother's perky, upbeat tone. "Did she weep that the past four years of stepmotherly love and dedication haven't won your heart?" She clasps her hands to her chest and fakes a sob.

Mina thrives on the noxious air that lingers above an emotional battlefield. Sometimes I do, too. Last night, after two hours of *Nutcracker* rehearsal with Ivon the Destroyer of feet and souls—the guest director Madisonville City Ballet brought in for this year's production—I was ready to create some drama of my own. I tasted the metallic flavor of trouble on my tongue as Mina and I drafted the blackmail letter, and I enjoyed it.

I strive for neutrality and balance in most things, but where the mothers in my life are concerned, I mostly try not to give in to the urge to poison their non-dairy creamer.

Both my mom and stepmom, Penelope, are lactose intolerant. It's the only thing they have in common aside from marrying my dad. Both make my life difficult—Mom because she can't be bothered, Penny because she bothers too much.

"I didn't give it to her. I decided to wait," I tell Mina. "See how it goes."

"What!"

"It's almost Christmas break. I'll be stuck in the house alone with her for days while Dad's at work. If she's upset, she'll mope around acting pathetic and I'll feel awful."

"She's going to convince your dad you're too young to go, and you'll lose your spot if you wait much longer to pay the deposit." Mina ambles deeper into the bus, standing on tiptoe to hunt for two empty seats next to each other. But the senior boys in front of us are tall and wide and taking their sweet time. She turns back to me. "You've got to show her you're not going to let her ruin your life."

I sigh. Missing the eight-week resident dance camp at the New York City College of Arts next summer probably won't ruin my life, but it won't help my career either. Mina and I are still just sophomores, but dancers need to be ready to go to work straight out of high school, or sooner. There are sixteen-year-olds working in professional ballet companies across the country.

Not that I want to be a ballet dancer. I have different goals, goals I will never tell Mina. Our supposed mutual desire to bleed into our toe shoes for a living is the glue that holds our friendship together.

My only friendship. I don't feel the need for more, but I don't want to lose Mina. Despite her flaws, she's a good friend. Loyal, but lacking that craving for extreme intimacy I've noticed in other best friend relationships. We tell each other many things, but not everything. I like that. It feels…safe.

"You know she's the one calling the shots, not your dad, right? I mean, that's not cool. She's not even really related to you."

"I know," I say. "I'll think of something. I just…I didn't feel right about it after I got home."

Bitching to Mina about Penny secretly slipping her loser brother hundreds of dollars every month is one thing. Threatening Penny with exposure is another. Penny is a pain, but she looks out for me in her control-freak kind of way. And she can't help lying to my dad. He doesn't believe in charity for family members. My stepmom is just trying to do what she feels she has to do for her brother while keeping her husband happy. No matter how much I resent her constantly sticking her nose into the business of "parenting" me—from her psychotic attention to my nutrition to the forced-fun family hiking trips—I still feel a certain amount of sympathy for her.

After all, haven't I told my share of lies in the name of keeping Dad happy?

"You're too good," Mina says. "It's a problem."

My lips thin, crooking at the edges. "I'll work on finding my inner evil."

"You do that." She gives the boys dawdling in the aisle in front of us another nasty look and flicks the ballet-shoe key chain hanging from my backpack zipper. "I hear Christmas spectaculars are great places to connect with inner evil."

"Probably. Santa's pretty scary when you think about it."

"Totally scary. Do we really have to go? Haven't you seen the Rockettes' crotches enough by now?"

Anxiety tightens the skin at my neck, making me regret buttoning the top button of my shirt. "I like the Rockettes."

"Really?"

"Really."

No, not really. I don't like the Rockettes, I *love* the Rockettes. It's a shameful secret I'll never tell anyone in my snobby dancer world, but I *love* them. Love them so much I want to be one. Forget toe shoes; give me tap shoes and high kicks.

Mina would die if she knew. So would my dad. Ballet as a career choice is bad enough, but at least it's "culturally relevant."

"Aren't we a little old for Radio City?"

I shrug. "Maybe, but we already signed up for the Christmas show. You know how Mrs. Martin is about changing things. She'll never let us switch."

"Fine." Mina rolls her eyes and my throat unclenches.

"But next year we're going to the Met." She turns around and stomps one boot on the floor. The boy in front of her—a senior with super-wavy brown hair, but the kind of face that can pull off Shirley Temple curls—glances over his shoulder and grins.

Despite her scary factor, Mina is very, very pretty.

"What's the problem, Nate?" Mina asks, a perfect mix of flirtation and annoyance in her tone.

I'm not surprised that she knows the guy's name. Madisonville Prep is divided into a girls' campus and a boys' campus, but we all get together for field trips and dances and charity stuff. In the past two years, Mina has made it her business to know the names of every decent-looking guy at Madisonville and dated more than a handful of them.

She dragged me along only once. The double date ended less than an hour after it began. I was too nervous to say a word to the boy her date had brought along for me. He bailed after coffee, before we even made it to the all-ages '80s night at the Den.

I think his name was Shane, but I can't really remember. I've tried to block his name and face from my memory, the better to not blush bright red the next time I see him.

He isn't on the trip today, I know that much.

"Krista and her minions are taking forever." Nate nods toward the rear of the bus, where a clutch of senior girls are arranging pillows and blankets and tiny portable televisions all connected to one laptop via a web of cords. The drive into the city only takes two hours, but they look like they're settling in for a transatlantic flight.

"Fabulous. Wonder what we're watching this time? *Twilight, New Moon,* or *Eclipse*?" Mina rolls her eyes again. Her eyeliner makes them look even more intensely blue. Really pretty. I can tell Nate notices, but doesn't notice me noticing him. People usually don't.

"I'm not watching anything." He slides into the seat on his left. "I'm going to sleep. You can sit with me if you want." He nods to the empty space beside him.

He's trying to keep it casual, but I can tell he's interested in Mina. I wonder if it's just because she's pretty or if he's heard the stories. According to legend, Mina is "great in bed." I don't know if that's true or not. Mina and I don't talk about things like that.

I think she can tell that sex mystifies me and that I prefer to stay mystified. It doesn't matter that I'll be sixteen in June. Sex is an adult thing to me. Maybe it's because I'm so thin and flat-chested that I still feel like a kid despite my height. Maybe it's because imagining being naked, skin to skin, with another human being makes my flesh crawl.

As far as I can tell, touching, hugging—closeness in general—is overrated. I prefer to be inviolate, alone in my body, without anyone trying to bridge the gap between one person and another. Skin was created for a reason, to keep us from getting too close. I don't see a reason to force something that seems unnatural.

I had enough forced closeness when I was little, when

dozens of doctors and nurses with their cold tools and colder hands took for granted the fact that they could touch me however they liked.

"Oh really?" Mina leans a hip against the seat. Her skirt inches up, revealing even more of her thigh. "So I get to watch you sleep all the way to New York? Sounds fun."

Oh no. She wouldn't. Would she?

Nate smiles. "I'm cute when I sleep."

"Who told you that?" Mina shifts closer. My teeth grind together. She wouldn't. She wouldn't leave me to sit by myself. She knows I don't have anyone else.

"My mom." Nate blinks big brown eyes, wondering if Mina will get the joke.

Low laughter, a purr of approval, slips from Mina's lips and curls on the seat next to Nate. Mina follows it a second later. "Fine, but if you snore and drool I'm recording it and posting it on YouTube."

Panic dumps into my bloodstream and goes swimming through my veins, tightening my throat, curling my fingers, making my bladder ache even though I used the bathroom just before getting on the bus. The few feet of emptiness in front of me, where Mina and Nate were standing a second ago, stretches on for miles.

The girl behind me shoves at my shoulders with her hot breath.

I have to go, find another seat, but I can't get my feet to move.

"You don't mind, do you, Dani?" Mina's blue eyes meet mine, wondering if I get the message. I do. I'm not nearly as oblivious as she thinks I am. She's angry that I didn't give Penny that letter, frustrated by the fact that I'm making her go see the Rockettes for the third year in a row.

This is my punishment.

I shake my head, tongue too thick to form words. Thankfully, my feet begin to move on their own, shuffling down the aisle. I reach the web of senior-girl wires and have to focus on stepping up and over, guiding my large feet safely down on the other side. The action calms me. Dance steps; it's just like choreographed dance steps, a series of organized movements that will take me where I need to go, to the prearranged place on stage. There is no uncertainty, no need to be afraid.

I pretend I'm back in the theater, inhaling the scent of old plaster and aging wood, scuffing my toe shoes through the chalk near the curtain to keep from slipping on the slick, worn planks of the stage. I move smoothly with the other dancers of the corps de ballet in front of me, each of us dressed for practice in identical pink tights and black leotards, each one with hair slicked tight into a bun, virtually indistinguishable except for our varying heights.

When I'm a Rockette, even that will fade away. Rockettes all have to be between five six and five ten and a half and are arranged on stage in such a way that the audience barely notices the slight difference. They are costumed alike, makeupped alike, trained and creatively padded so that even their bodies seem identical.

And when they dance, they dance as one entity, in

harmony, consuming the attention of every last person in their world while still remaining individually invisible.

Invisible, but seen. Anonymous, but beloved.

Sometimes my dream seems the stupidest thing in the world. Sometimes it is a secret treasure in my pocket.

My hands tremble on the worn leather of the seats on either side of the aisle, my eyes stare at the back window and the red emergency handle underneath. I've reached the end of the line.

"You okay?"

I turn toward the voice. It belongs to a boy, one I recognize, but not one of Mina's conquests. Mina only pretends to be bad. In reality she has to be in by eleven, goes to mass every Sunday with her family, and babysits her two little half-brothers every Wednesday night so her mom and stepdad can have their "date night." She's never written a letter telling her stepdad she hates the way he says mean things about her biological father, she's never snuck out her ground-floor window, and she's never talked back to a teacher or turned in her homework a day late or worn her hair down to ballet class.

Her biggest act of defiance is perpetrated with an eyeliner pencil.

Not so with this boy. He is genuinely Bad. He was suspended twice last year, once for punching an assistant coach during lacrosse practice. At the time, everyone was certain he would be expelled for good. He's a scholarship student. They're expected to be on their best behavior, grateful for the gift they've been given. And even if his family was a top contributor to Madisonville Prep, there's a strict "no violence" policy. We aren't allowed to hit *each other*, let alone a teacher—even if he is just an assistant coach.

But come August, there he was, Jesse Vance in the flesh, hunched over the extracurricular activities registration table, signing up for the fall after-school sports programs. His short black hair stuck straight in the air the way it always had, his bright blue eyes were sharp and watchful, alien in a room full of people who had never considered whether they were predators or prey.

Well…most hadn't considered it. If I let myself, I could remember. There's a reason I play the diabetes card to get out of anything resembling a competitive sport in gym class.

Not so with Jesse. He plays every sport known to man and is extraordinary at every one. He's six feet tall and built like a grown man, strong and solid and terrifying. I've seen what his body can do to other boys on the wrestling team, watched the contained violence in the way he wields his lacrosse stick.

We all suspect that athletic promise is the reason he was allowed to stay, though he's probably dangerous and undoubtedly scary.

Jesse doesn't have a single friend at Madisonville Prep. He's the only boy I've ever seen who can play with a team, but not seem a part of it. He doesn't joke or smile with the other boys, he doesn't date any of the girls. He's an outsider in every sense of the word. I see him on the town commons at least once a week, but he's always alone. Not even the rougher, cooler, townie kids will come anywhere near him.

He might as well have yellow caution tape floating around his body.

"Are you okay?"

And he's asking if I'm okay.

"Dani?"

And he knows my name.

His eyes slide to the front of the bus then back to me. "Sit down." His hand closes around my wrist, completely encircling the bone. I have small bones, but his hands are huge. His fingers and thumb overlap, beginning a second journey around my arm. My diabetic bracelet slips down to brush against his skin, but he doesn't seem to notice.

Good. I don't like people to know if I can help it. My diabetes is mild compared to what it was when I was a kid, but still…it's something I like to keep secret. To ignore. Even as I make a mental note to eat the muffin in my backpack before too much longer, before the insulin shot I gave myself a few minutes ago in the bathroom kicks in, I manage to largely ignore the mathematics associated with diabetes management.

There is no ignoring the fact that Jesse is touching me. He's looking up into my eyes, expecting an answer. Expecting action.

If someone had told me this was going happen, I would have been terrified. My panic attack after Mina's dismissal would have faded to a tiny tremor on my radar in comparison to the earthquake of this interaction. A boy is *touching* me, and not just any boy, but Jesse Vance.

But this crept up on me unaware, this moment of being tugged down into the empty seat next to Jesse. His hand is warm and firm, but strangely gentle. It's as if he knows how ridiculously hard the solo dance to the back of the bus was for me, as if he understands what it feels like to be breakable.

"It's the last empty seat." His tone is dismissive, but his fingers linger on my wrist before pulling away. He crosses his arms and turns toward the window, but his shoulders are so broad that his body still brushes against mine.

The place where we touch has a mini panic attack of its own. The skin beneath my sweater burns hot then cold, the nerve endings shredding and reforming themselves in the wake of this shocking new discovery.

The discovery that maybe separation isn't as desirable as I'd thought, that maybe, just maybe, the gaps between people are meant to be bridged.

Two.

Jesse

For a second, I think about grabbing her and making a run for it. We could be out the back of the bus and into the woods behind the school before anyone notices we're gone. The alarm doesn't work. This is the same bus the lacrosse team uses for away games, and Coach disabled the alarm last spring so we could load our duffle bags and equipment from the back without listening to the thing scream. Dani and I could go. Run. Hide.

I could force her to come with me.

She's tall, but thin. Physically strong—I could feel it when I grabbed her wrist—but emotionally weak. She almost lost it when her friend ditched her. She won't fight or call for help. And when I tell her the truth, she might even believe me.

Dani isn't like the others. I can tell she knows what it's like to be afraid. She knows how many things there are to be afraid of.

"Thanks." Her voice is deeper than I thought it would

be, but pretty. It sounds like she'd be a good singer. "I'm Dani…guess you know that."

Of course I know. She's pale and a little too skinny and never wears a skirt or makeup, but she's one of the prettiest girls at Madisonville Prep. Not hot, but beautiful in a simple kind of way. Her big brown eyes see everything and her hair is shiny like those girls in the shampoo commercials. I've always wondered if it's as soft as it looks. It would have to be pretty soft to compete with her skin. Her skin was like tissue paper. I could feel the flutter of her pulse underneath it. I can still smell the soap and mint and flowers mixing in her perfume.

Or maybe it's just shampoo. She doesn't seem like the type who wears perfume. She doesn't try that hard. It's part of what makes her interesting.

Most people at Mad Prep don't notice Dani, but I knew her name and basic details a few days after I enrolled. I know she has a pretty, blond stepmom who picks her up after school and a big deal doctor dad who is a Major Donor. I know that she's some kind of dancer and that she would be one of the first people signed up for this stupid field trip.

I knew all that even before the man with her picture slipped me five hundred dollars to make sure she got on this bus.

I wasn't planning to go to New York before that. It's the last day of school before break; who wants to make it any longer than it has to be? Especially to go to a museum or some musical with one hundred dancing Santa Clauses or whatever the hell that Radio City thing is about.

Madisonville Prep dismisses at three forty-five; the bus from New York City won't be back until after eight at night. It's a no-brainer. It's better to stay at school and watch a bunch of dumb movies or sleep in classes where the teachers couldn't care less what you do now that finals are over, and be free four hours earlier.

But then, last Tuesday, the man gave me the money. Five hundred dollars. More money than I've ever held at once.

I go to an expensive school on scholarship and I live with people who've never earned more than twenty grand a year and don't like spending much of it on me. Even the money the government gives them for allowing me to live there. I pay for a lot of my own food, and buy my own clothes and uniforms with money I earn working construction during the summer. I break my back for three months so I can spend the school year breaking the rest of the bones in my body. Playing three sports doesn't leave much time for an after-school job.

My counselors at school say it will all be worth it in the end. I have decent grades, but I have star potential as an athlete. I'll get a scholarship, change my life, and finally become something more than a foster kid or an "abuse survivor." I'm a big deal. Scouts are already noticing, even though I'm just a junior.

At first, I thought the man was a college scout.

He was wearing a green warm-up suit, glasses, and

a ball hat. He hung around for our entire soccer game against Ithaca High School, even when it started to rain halfway through. Most of the parents had gone to sit in their cars by the end, but the guy stayed. And gave me money to go on a field trip. And to make sure Danielle Connor went on it, too.

"You're Jesse, right?" She picks at the skin around her cuticle. I can see her fingers out of the corner of my eye. I'm making her nervous.

Still, I don't say anything. I don't know what to say.

Run. We have to get off this bus.

She'll think I'm crazy. Maybe I am. Maybe nothing is going to happen.

Right. Some old man in dark glasses gives you money to make sure a pretty girl gets on a school bus going to a big city. Nothing's going to happen, there's no way he's going to grab her and lock her in some basement room and do things to her.

Things even worse than they did to you.

The bus rumbles and lurches forward. I smell fuel and my stomach clenches. My fingers dig into my own arms. It's too late now.

It's always too late.

Sweat gathers between my shoulder blades. I drop my forehead to the cold window and suck in a breath, watching trees become houses and houses become fast food restaurants and fast food restaurants fade into trees again as we merge onto the highway heading south. The sun is shining so bright the frost in the fields on the side of the road makes my eyes hurt. It's a perfect day and everything is going to be fine.

Everything really is going to be fine. I signed up for the stupid Radio City show. I'll follow Dani and her friend and sit a few rows behind. If she gets up to go to the bathroom, I'll go with her. If she and her friend go shopping, I'll go too. I'll be their shadow, ready to kick that man's ass if he shows up and tries to grab Dani. I'm bigger than he is. Unless he has a gun, there's no way he'll be able to take me.

I pocketed the money before I thought better of it, but I've thought better of it now.

Anyway, I did what he asked me to do. I made sure Dani's name was on the sign-up list and I added mine in the last space. We're both on the bus heading for New York City. I never told the freak I'd let him abduct her or touch her or even look at her up close.

Close. We're close. Our shoulders brush just the slightest bit. She doesn't pull away the way I think she will, but I know she can't be comfortable. I've never seen her touch anyone except that goth girl she's friends with, and she doesn't have a boyfriend. At lacrosse practice last year, Gareth said he thought she was a lesbian. He wasn't being mean about it, just making an observation, but I've remembered it ever since.

I'd bet my leg that Danielle doesn't like girls like that. But she doesn't like guys, either. She doesn't like people, at least not when they get too close. She needs her space. She's like me. I felt it from the second I first saw her, and every careful step she took to get to the back of the bus was a spy confirming my suspicions.

I suddenly want to know what happened to her to make her like me. But then just as quickly decide I don't. I have enough bad memories of my own; I don't need to collect someone else's.

Still, I never imagined we'd end up sitting next to each other. It never entered my mind. I wonder if it's a sign that my gut is right and I need to watch out for her. If so, it would be a good idea to quit acting like an asshole. Otherwise, she'll be as scared of me as some stalker old enough to be her dad.

Just ask her what she's doing over break, or tell her you like the smell of her—

No, don't tell her that. You don't talk to a girl like Dani about the way she smells. Tell her you've seen her around school. Ask her what grade she's in. Tell her you—

Say "hi," idiot. Say "what's up?" Something! Or just turn and look at her. Quit staring at the window like a loser or it's going to be too late.

Too late. I see the headlights coming, but my brain doesn't register what they are until after. They're too high, too intense. Even in the early morning sunlight, they're bright enough to blind me. I squint and turn to Dani, planning to ask her if she knows what they are.

I've barely turned away from the window when the semi hits.

The middle of the bus explodes, glass shattering, metal groaning as people near the point of impact are thrown from their seats. Dani and I are forced the other direction as the two ends of the bus fold back around the truck.

Dani crashes into me, her light body slamming against mine. My arms close around her on instinct just before the back of my head hits the window. I can hear the pop of bone striking glass over the cries of the girls in front of us and the wail of iron as the bus screeches across the road. My brain feels soft and squishy and the day grows darker, like somebody turned down the sun.

Dani's hands clutch mine as she curls into a ball. She's smarter than I am; some part of her must have known we wouldn't be smashed against the glass for long.

Our sideways movement ends in a moment of horrible stillness. One second we're skidding, then, with a groan and a crack, we're falling. Faster, faster, off the side of the bridge, shooting through empty air.

The world whirls and people fly like clothes in a dryer, flipping over each other, feet and hands and jackets and backpacks and portable televisions colliding and coming apart broken. I curl around Dani, clenching my stomach and tucking my head, trying to protect as much of her as possible. I've already got a busted skull; might as well put my broken body to use.

We start to fall toward the opposite window, but by the time we get to the other side, the window is the roof of the bus. My spine hits—hard. I make a noise, but I can't hear it over the rushing of the blood in my head. Maybe it's because of the injury; maybe it's a side effect of fear.

I've never been so afraid. The world is sharp with it;

everything stands out like a scene from a pop-out book. I swear I can see pupils dilate, pieces of dirt rise up from the floor as gravity reverses its pressure, concrete rush by smashed windows with teeth made of broken glass.

Then it's over, ending with a bang way bigger than the one it started with.

The bus lands on the same side it was hit, the force of our fall knocking the bus flat again, ironing out the wrinkle made by the initial impact. As metal and rubber and glass collide with cold earth, a collective groan fills the air, a sound of such pure pain it makes my teeth hurt.

Or maybe they hurt because Dani's skull slams into my jaw as we land. She groans and goes limp just before we slide down the side of the roof to puddle with the rest of the bodies on the new floor.

I smell gasoline and sewer. I feel the cold winter day seeping into the air, cooling the blood that spills from torn skin.

God, everything hurts. My ribs, my head, my arms, my jaw. Glass slices into my side and stabs through my sweater and undershirt, but I can't move. There's a terrible pressure in my chest and a something…

Something…crooked…rattles inside my brain.

More gasoline stink, so strong I can almost taste it. Visions of big-budget movie crashes and cars going up in a burst of flames shoot behind my eyes. My foster dad says that's a bunch of Hollywood bullshit. Real cars hardly ever burn. He ought to know, he drives a tow truck part-time.

Only part-time, so he can spend the rest of his time on the couch watching those bad movies.

When I was younger, before Mad Prep and the endless soccer and wrestling and lacrosse practices, I used to watch them with him. I never realized I missed those long, lazy nights until this very second. I'll have to tell Trent that he isn't a complete loser. I didn't always consider every day under his roof another day in prison.

In fact, in those early days, watching movies with him probably saved my life. The later I stayed up, the less time I had to spend in my bed waiting for the monster that kept trying to kill me. Green and black, with slick scales covering snakelike muscles—the monster was every bad dream I'd ever had rolled into one terrifying package.

I never got a good look at the creature, but I felt its death grip around my neck dozens of times. I smelled its devil breath and watched its red eyes glow in the darkness. It would hover over me while I slept, but never strike until it knew I was awake. It wanted me to be conscious when I died, wanted to lick up my fear with its rough tongue, soak up my death like bread swiped through spaghetti sauce.

In my mind, I called it the Thing, but I never named it aloud. I never said a word, never made a sound, never cried out for help. I knew by then that crying out for help only worked if there was someone around who gave a damn. I stopped calling out and learned how to fight. And I fought and I fought, every single night, until finally the monster went away. Around my tenth birthday.

It's been seven years since I've seen the Thing. It's been almost that long since I've thought about it. Even when I push myself to the breaking point in the weight room, getting bigger, stronger, meaner than anyone else, I don't let myself wonder why I need to be so strong. Even when I go to sleep with the lights and the television on, I don't let myself remember why I'm afraid of the dark.

I don't admit to anyone—even myself—that I'm afraid of anything.

But I am. I'm afraid of dying in this bus. I'm afraid of Dani dying in my arms. I'm afraid of the Thing that came in the night, the Thing I almost swear I can see curled around the broken steering wheel at the front of the bus, staring down the long row of broken, moaning, twisted bodies.

Looking straight at me.

Three

Jesse

Red eyes sent from hell glare above the dragon's mouth and blood drips from its fangs. It leaps from the steering wheel, claws crunching in the broken glass. Green-and-black scales ripple over muscles way bigger than mine, thick masses of tissue that assure me that I'm as small and helpless as when I first went into the hospital.

It's the Thing, no doubt about it. I've never seen it in the daylight before, but I've felt that reptilian body crouched on top of me, tense and ready to strike.

"Mina...Mina." Dani shifts in my arms, eyelids fluttering. Her head turns and her blood smears onto my sweater.

The skin above her right cheek is split open, and red trickles down her face. I can almost feel how much the Thing would enjoy licking that trail away, getting a taste before coming in for the kill.

Kill. The Thing is back. It's here. It's *real*. And it could kill everyone on this bus.

Or at least everyone who isn't dead already.

The bus is mostly still now. Only a few pained moans and sobs break the silence. A couple of people at the front are moving—flailing arms and legs, struggling to sit up with no help from broken bones and bruised bodies—but the middle is silent. Dead silent.

The place where Dani's friend sat down is the hardest hit, just ahead of the point of impact where the seats are twisted beyond recognition. The chances that Mina is seriously hurt are good and getting better as the Thing slinks into the center of the bus, crawling over debris, pausing to survey the limp bodies with satisfaction. Its eyes slit and it pulls its bloodied lips back another inch, baring more of those impossibly large teeth.

"Mina…we have to…" Dani's eyes open, but almost immediately wince closed again. She shudders against me like it hurts to breathe. "I have to…"

We have to get out, that's what we have to do. We have to get the hell out of this bus and away from that dragon before we're as dead as half the student body of Madisonville Prep.

"Hold onto me." I scoop Dani into my arms, ignoring the sting in my side and the rush of warmth that seeps through my sweater, and fight my way to my feet.

What's left of the bus window shatters beneath our combined weight and my left leg plunges through the hole to sink into the muddy ground. I tug it free, gritting my teeth as one of the glass shards stabs into my calf and lodges there. I stumble back toward the emergency exit, feeling my way as I climb over the other seats, too scared to turn my back on the Thing.

"But what about—"

"The bus could explode," I say, realizing a part of me worries my words are true. The sharp smell of gasoline bites at my nose, making my already aching head spin. "We have to get out. We'll call for help when we're safe."

You'll never be safe. Never again. Never, never, never. It came for you in the daylight. It won't be leaving without your blood in its mouth.

I move faster, tripping over dead weight. *Dead weight.* People are dead, people I've seen every day, who I've envied for their easy smiles and simple problems. And now they're dead, and Dani and I could be next.

"My backpack…" Dani reaches a hand toward where we were sitting, but it falls back to her side a second later. Her head lolls against my shoulder. I glance down in time to see her eyes roll back and her lids flutter closed. She's losing consciousness again, maybe even dying.

"Dani, wake up, don't go to sleep. Stay awake!" The panic in my voice draws the attention of the monster.

Twenty feet away, the Thing hisses and crouches lower, wiggling its haunches, getting ready to pounce. Dani didn't see it and none of the people at the front of the bus seem to have noticed a nightmare the size of a small horse slinking through the wreckage, but that doesn't stop my heart from kicking into adrenaline-fueled overdrive. I don't care if anyone else can see it. *I* can see it.

And I know if it gets close enough, I'll *feel* it.

Memories of fighting for my life—small hands clenching around that neck, straining to keep its teeth away from my face, wrestling for hours in hot, sticky sheets and waking up in the morning with bruises on my ribs—convince me it's time to risk turning my back on danger in the name of getting the hell out of here. Now.

I spin and lunge for the now-horizontal emergency door. Amazingly, it is still whole and clinging to its rusted hinges. All I have to do is get my hands on the handle and push. Two more steps and we're there. I lift my foot, aiming for the center of the door. My boot is only seconds away from impact when I see it.

I jerk my knee to my chest and scream, a raw, terrified sound that stirs up echoes from the front of the bus. But the people up there are only responding to my fear. They have no idea what they're screaming about. There's no way they could. They can't see the Thing from up there. It isn't in the bus with us anymore. It's outside, clawing at the glass that separates its fangs from my foot. I'd nearly let it back in and delivered Dani right into its jaws.

My heart slams in my chest as I back away.

How did it get outside so fast? And how am I ever going to outrun it, even if I do find another way out?

Hours of sprints up and down the soccer field haven't prepared me for this. I was an idiot to think I could ever be big enough or strong enough that I wouldn't have to be afraid. I will always be afraid. Until the day I die. Until the day this monster kills me.

The Thing lunges. Its face smashes into the glass,

sending a crack shivering up the center. A few more hits like that and it'll be on top of us.

"Shit!" Blood rushes to my head. Fear and the smell of gasoline—so much thicker here in the very back of the bus—is making me dizzy. I stumble and Dani cries out, but it takes me a second to realize I'm the reason she's in pain. I'm holding her too tight.

I force my hands to relax and my feet to move. I pick my way back over the last seat and across the still forms of Bart Stevens and Na Ngyuen, the only two people socially awkward enough to end up closer to the back than Dani and me. The rest of the bus looms in front of me, an obstacle course filled with bleeding people and crushed seats and a jumble of backpacks and sack lunches and iPods, all useless now that there will be no one alive to use them. Hopelessness catches in my throat, making it hard to swallow. It's too far. We'll never make it before the bus goes up in flames.

I can smell it now, above the gasoline and the wet earth of the riverbed. Sour ash and burning rubber. Smoke. Somewhere outside, the bus is on fire. Even if that B movie explosion I've been imagining since we crashed doesn't happen, this bus is going to burn and we'll all burn right along with our unnecessary possessions if we don't get out.

"Get out of the bus!" I yell, voice pinging off the crushed metal walls. "Get out! Get as far away as you can! The bus is on fire."

"Fire!" Someone sobs the word, stirring up another

round of fear-echoes, but I don't wait around to see if the few conscious people take my advice. I turn back to the emergency exit and the dragon that waits for me with its red eyes and bloody teeth, and I run.

I slam into the handle with my side and jump, legs churning through the air, hoping to get some distance between me and the bus. I hit the ground hard, muscles clenching around the shard still stuck in my calf. Agony jolts up my leg and I cry out, but I don't stop. I don't dare look back to see if the monster I've cleared is already coming after me. I just run. I run as fast as I can, faster than I would have thought possible with glass in my leg, a sliced-up side, and carrying another person. Dani can't weigh more than a hundred and twenty pounds—a hundred thirty at most. Still, it's a lot more weight than I'm used to.

But you wouldn't know it by the way my feet eat up the sandy ground between the bus and the concrete pillars of the bridge. I'm Vince Young in the 2006 Rosebowl, I'm Superman on speed, so fast the wind stings my eyes and makes tears run down my cheeks. If the college scouts were watching, I'd score a fat scholarship on the spot.

Instead, I make an even bigger score. I keep Dani and me alive for a few more minutes.

The explosion rips through the air, filling the world, booming through the narrow riverbed. It crashes into my ears, rattling the loose piece in my brain. The heat comes a second later, burning against my back, so hot I start to sweat even though the front of my body is freezing cold.

The bus exploded. It really did, just like I was afraid it would.

Wouldn't Trent have loved to see that?

It's my last thought before something hits the back of my head and more warm blood spills down my neck. The gray light filtering into the riverbed flares white, then yellow, and then blackness sweeps in. I fall, the arms holding Dani clenching one last time before my vision snuffs out.

Dani

So tired, so cold. But still, I'm sweating. My forehead and upper lip are freckled with little beads, just like when we have ballet rehearsal in the theater during the summer.

The owner insists a theater in upstate New York doesn't need air conditioning. Maybe that's true at night— when the temperatures drop and the patrons come inside wearing sweaters and jackets they can take off if they get too warm—but for the dancers practicing in the eighty-degree heat of midday, it's stifling. My leotard is always drenched and sticky by the first break.

But I'm not wearing a leotard now. I'm in my school uniform. It's the crisp cotton of my white button-up that's glued to my clammy skin, not the soft fabric of my ancient dancewear. And I'm not inside…I'm outside. Cold, winter air stirs the hair on my neck, trying to freeze the drops sliding into my collar into sweat-cicles.

What am I doing outside? And why does my body hurt all over?

With way more effort than something so simple should require, I open my eyes. I catch a glimpse of rocks and dirt before my lids slam closed, shutters made of lead.

Where am I? What happened? And why can't I keep my eyes open?

Images tease at the edges of my brain—glass shattering, wide, frightened mouths, strong arms that hold me tight as the world spins—but I can't seem to hold on to the pictures long enough to make sense of their message. I am so tired. So, *so* very tired. Too tired to think, too tired to talk, too tired to stay awake.

Stay awake. Jesse. He told me to stay awake. He was holding me, carrying me out of the wrecked bus, trying to save my life. But now I'm sprawled on cold sand.

Dread jolts my heart like an electric shock and my eyes flicker open. The bus. The accident. What if Jesse didn't make it out, what if—

"Dani?" His face appears above mine, blue eyes as bright as the clear winter sky behind him, triggering a grateful squeeze in my chest.

He's alive! It feels like I've been given some priceless gift. Crazy, since I hardly know him, but maybe not *that* crazy. He saved my life. I was dead weight, but he picked me up and carried me with him when he could have jumped out of the bus and saved himself. "Are you okay? I just woke up. I don't know how long we've been out. Can you hear me?"

"Mm…hrrss…" In my head the words are clear, but

they come out muffled and strange. I try again to tell him I'm okay, but my lips won't cooperate. "Nee…mmmm."

"Don't try to talk." He winces as he slides one arm beneath my shoulder and helps me sit. Before I can get accustomed to the feel of his arms around me, of my elbow crooked around his neck, the world spins. I catch a dizzy glimpse of smoke and fire as Jesse's other arm slips beneath my knees, and then he's lifting me off the ground. Over his shoulder, ribbons of red and orange snake through the frigid air.

The bus. It's on fire. It really *did* explode. Mina and Nate and all the other kids and Mrs. Martin and the bus driver—the same old man who drove the bus for every field trip for as long as I can remember—are burning. Maybe while they're still alive, trapped and unable to escape.

The realization sends another jolt through my body, chasing some of the lethargy away.

"We have to…get help." I twist in Jesse's arms as he turns and stumbles away from the wreckage.

"I told them to get out. We can't do anything else. We have to keep running. I don't know when it's going to come back." His voice is strong and sure, even though what he's saying verges on nonsense. "I don't know why it didn't get me while I was passed out, but it'll be back. I know it will. It's not going to stop this time."

Paranoid nonsense.

He's probably in shock, a fact that would con-sume more of my attention if my arm didn't choose that moment to snap into my chest and stay there, twitching, for several seconds. Even my muddled brain knows what this means. Involuntary muscles spasms, the cold sweat, the light feeling in my head, the lethargy, the inability to think straight—I've felt all of these things before. When I was younger and my diabetes was totally out of control, I suffered insulin reactions all the time.

But back then, I always had a doctor or a nurse or at least a grown-up close by who knew about my condition. And I kept a roll of lifesavers in my pocket, prepared to give my sugar a boost when I needed it. I still keep a roll in my backpack, along with my shots and blood sugar monitor.

But my backpack's not here. It's burning on that bus, right along with my best friend.

"Mina! We have to go back. We have to help—"

"We can't help. Anyone who was alive after the crash is dead now. We have to go!"

His words make my throat burn. I taste the orange juice I had first thing this morning. Orange juice. I'll think about orange juice instead of Mina, instead of all the other scary things I need to think about. For once, concentrating on the math of carbs-versus-insulin is a blessing.

I close my eyes, visualizing the cool glass of juice. I only had a few sips. That's all. Then the shot in the bathroom before Mina and I got in line for the field trip. The bus crashed before I had the chance to unwrap the muffin I'd intended to eat. Now, I'll get progressively sicker unless I get something in my system. It's actually amazing I'm not worse than I am already. But I definitely can't let Jesse drag me out into the middle of nowhere. I have to stay by the bus and hope an ambulance and trained medical professionals get to me in time.

"Wait…I'm diabetic. I have to stay by the bus." I manage to get the words out with only a slight slur. I know Jesse has to have heard me, but he doesn't stop walking away. In fact, he breaks into a hobbled run, a jog-hop that jolts my aching head with every step. "Please, I need sugar. You have to stop. Please, I—"

"I can't stop. I'm sorry. I just can't." He shakes his head and casts an anxious look over his shoulder. "And I can't leave you there. It could hurt you. It could be real."

The words prick at something inside of me, that part that knows what it's like to be afraid for no reason, to be out of your mind believing in things that aren't there, *people* who aren't there.

I haven't thought about Rachel in years. Dreamt about her, woken up screaming with her ruined face burned onto my mental screen—yes. But I haven't consciously thought about her. I've done my best to erase those memories, to wall them up inside my mind and let them suffocate from lack of oxygen.

But now the wreck, the fear, the smell of smoke, and the horrible ache in my head…

The walls are crumbling. I can almost sense Rachel slipping out, stealing out of her prison with a *tap tap tap* of her best dress-up shoes.

No. She's not real. You're just going into shock. You need food.

I shiver; the sweat on my neck feels like someone is holding an ice cube to my bare skin. "I need sugar," I say. "I have to eat or I'll get really sick. I'm diabetic." I hold my bracelet in front of his face and watch as understanding creeps across his features.

His incredibly handsome features. Even now, even afraid and delirious, the strange temptation of his skin remains. I want to trace the strong line of his jaw, feel if his lips are as soft as they look. When my hand drops, it doesn't fall back into my lap. It moves to his chest, feathering over where his muscles clench tight beneath his sweater. It's all the confirmation I need that I'm not in my right mind. If I were, I would never dare to press against him, to explore the place where his chest bone becomes muscle with my fingers.

"Okay…okay," he mutters beneath his breath, not seeming to notice my touch though he pulls me closer. "So you need to eat? You don't need…a shot or something?"

"I took my insulin before I got on the bus. I just need some candy or juice, some kind of sugar or I'll get sick."

But even as I speak, saying things I know are true, I can't help but notice how much easier it is to form words than it was a second before. Except for the odd rattled feeling in my head, I'm starting to feel better, not worse…which doesn't make sense.

Jesse slows, but doesn't turn around. "Okay. I know

a place we can go. It's not too far, and I think they have food. They should, anyway. At least a Coke or something."

"Jesse, please. Just let me go back to the bus. I'm sure the police—"

"The police can't help. They might not even be able to…"

I watch him, watch his throat work as he swallows, and wonder what has made this big, bad boy so afraid. "Might not be able to what?" I ask.

"Nothing. You'll…think I'm crazy." His eyes are icy blue, but burning from the inside out. My arm that's still around his neck flexes, responding to the need to hold him without my conscious permission. "You probably think I'm crazy already."

I should, but I don't. He isn't crazy, he's just…scared. Scared half to death, the way I've been scared for most of my life. There's something about being afraid of a monster no one else believes in, that no one else can even *see*, that pushes fear into the realm of mind-blowing terror. That kind of terror destroys things inside you, things necessary to leading a normal life.

But how can you ever be normal when you know that the terrors under the bed are real, that they want your blood on their "imaginary" hands?

The thought has barely whispered through my mind when I see the flash of shining brown hair and sparkling blue eyes in the bare tree limbs above my head.

Rachel. She's back.

Four

Dani

"Run! We have to run!" My fingers claw into Jesse's neck and my legs thrash. I know it's pointless to run when my feet aren't even on the ground, but I can't seem to stop. I'm not in control, not thinking straight. I can't think of anything but Rachel and her mean little eyes and the gaping red hole when she smiles.

Blood oozes from her mouth, dripping down onto the speckled bark of the tree limb beneath her. The branch is thick and ancient, making Rachel seem even more petite by comparison, a doll lost in the woods.

I've grown up, but Rachel hasn't. She's still a kid, no more than eight or nine, still wearing that brown dress with the white bow and the matching white leather shoes. Now—from my vantage point far below—I can see she even wears ruffled white panties beneath her dress, the kind my mother bought me when I was four. She's all innocence and little girl frills.

Except for that mouth. That horror of a mouth that spills death into the air.

A drop of red falls from the tree, passing inches from my face, landing on the back of Jesse's hand, making me scream. And scream and scream and scream. It's really there. I can see the blood smearing through the brown hairs, already starting to dry a darker crimson.

Rachel is here. She's real. She's back, and she's going to prove that all my nightmares weren't bad dreams, but prophecies. She's going to kill me. Finally, finally, finally, just when I was stupid enough to think I was safe.

"What's wrong?" Jesse has to yell to be heard over the screams. The screams I can't seem to stop, no matter how hard I try. "Dani? What's—"

The tree splinters, louder than Jesse's words, louder than my screams. Thank God, Jesse hears it too. His head snaps up, spotting the massive limb just as it begins to fall. He dives forward, throwing me onto the riverbed. I land with a groan. Rocks dig into my hips and knees as I roll to a stop, but there isn't any real damage done.

Jesse isn't so lucky.

The tree lands on his leg, pinning him to the ground. He cries out, an animal sound that rattles me more than my tumble across the rocks. Rachel's attack has hit a mark. Maybe not the mark she intended, but I have a feeling Rachel doesn't care about collateral damage. The only good news is that she's gone, vanished into thin air the way she often did in the past after an especially intense attempt on my life.

Still, she could be back any second. We aren't safe here; we have to get to a more populated area. Rachel never came for me when other people were around. It was always when I was alone, late at night when everyone who was supposed to be watching me was too tired to bother.

But she came now. In the middle of the morning, with Jesse standing right there.

I shove the thought aside. I can't think about that now, I can't let myself believe there is no safe place. "Jesse! Are you okay?" I stand on wobbly legs and hurry to his side.

I would like to think I would have gone back to him even if Rachel were still dancing on the bloodied bark she left behind, but I can't know for sure. The fear is still too fresh, swelling inside me, filling every empty place with blind, heart-pounding terror.

Rachel. Rachel is back. She's back, and not playing by the rules.

"I'm fine. Just a little bruised." Jesse's deep voice is deeper than usual, a pain-filled rumble that makes me more afraid.

Rachel has hurt a boy twice my size. The second my guard is down, she's going to take me out without breaking a sweat. My chin jerks up, scanning the rest of the trees near the river, heart racing as I search for a spot of red amid the gray and brown. She's up there somewhere; I can feel her, I can smell the scent of peppermint and salt and medicine that clings to her hair, I can—

"Dani. I need help." Something in Jesse's tone tells me this isn't the first time he's asked. "I need to get this thing off my leg before it breaks something."

My eyes snap back to his. "Right. Right." I nod until I realize I've nodded too long and stop myself with a clench of my jaw. Hold it together. I can hold it together. My trembling hands find the scratchy bark of the tree and push. Nothing. I gather my strength and push again, but the limb doesn't move an inch. "It's too heavy. I can't move it."

"Shit," he whispers. I turn to see his forehead pressed to the back of one hand, his eyes squeezed shut in pain or terror or a mixture of both. "I can't stay like this. It's not safe. I can't defend myself."

I sway a little on my feet. It almost sounds like he…like he saw…

"Did you see something? Up in the tree?" I slide down to sit by his trapped leg, clawing my fingers into the cold sand while I wait for his answer.

He's silent for a moment before turning to look at me over his shoulder. "No. I didn't see anything in the tree." It's the truth, but not the whole truth; the haunted look in his eyes assures me he knows that limb didn't fall on its own. "I didn't look up in time. What did you see?"

"I…" What can I say? What can I say that won't make me sound as nuts as he worried I'd find him? "No-nothing."

"Nothing made you scream like that?"

"No. I…sometimes…when my sugar is low…"

When my sugar is low.

That's it! Rachel isn't really back; I'm just starting to hallucinate. That's all this is. As soon as I get a Coke or a box of juice into my body, Rachel will vanish. She'll be walled back inside her prison in my mind and life will go back to normal.

Pretty lies, pretty lies, always with the pretty lies.

I whirl to search the tree limbs. I twist first to one side and then the other, scouring the riverbed for that brown dress. The voice I heard in my head wasn't mine. It was hers, Rachel's, that sing-song little girl's voice that once made me laugh. Now it makes me want to start screaming again. Instead, I bite my lip, afraid if I get going I'll never stop, that I'll scream until my brain turns to liquid and runs out my nose in a rush of red.

Red mouth, bloody lips. I should see them. She has to be close. But where is she? Why isn't she showing herself? How long do we have before the next attack?

"Dani? Can you hear me?" Jesse asks.

"Yes." But my voice is too soft, too far away from my ears. I have to get out of here. I have to get Jesse out of here. But how am I supposed to do that when I can barely lift the twelve-pound weights in gym class, let alone a couple hundred pounds of tree?

My fingers clench and suddenly I'm fisting two handfuls of sand. I look down, taking longer than I should to connect the dots. Sand. Hands. Freedom. "I can dig you out."

Jesse nods, relief in his eyes. "I'll help." He twists as much as he's able with one leg pinned, his big hand reaching down to join mine. Together we claw at the damp sand until our skin is coated with grit and our fingers cramped with cold, but finally—just as the faint echo of sirens pierce the air—we manage to create enough space for Jesse to tug his leg free.

I gasp when I see it. His khaki pants are shredded and bloody and a thick shard of glass protrudes from the pale skin of his calf. I reach for it without thinking and tug it free. Jesse flinches, and then flinches again when I press my fingers over the wound to stop the rush of blood.

"Thanks," he says. "That's better...I think."

"You're welcome," I whisper, staring at the glass on the ground, marveling that he was able to walk. My gaze slides back to my hands. The dark, nearly black hair on Jesse's legs is strangely intriguing, so springy and coarse under my fingers.

I've never seen a boy's bare leg so up-close-and-personal before. My father is the only man in our house and he wears a suit to work. Or scrubs if they're planning a messy batch of experiments. At home, he wears expensive pajama pants that my stepmom buys him on her trips to Europe and jeans on his days off, even in the summer. My father doesn't believe in showing his legs. I can't remember seeing them, not ever. I've certainly never touched them.

Not that touching my father would be at all similar to touching Jesse.

Touching Jesse...My hand twitches against his skin. *I* am touching Jesse. Through the fear and anxiety and the certainty that Rachel will return at any moment, the peculiarity of this sudden intimacy pierces my muddied thoughts. I blush, then blush harder as his hand reaches out to cover mine. Somehow, even after our dig through the freezing ground, his skin is still warm.

"Dani?" Now Jesse is touching *me*. I curl my fingers around his hand, feeling both safer and more anxious than I did a moment before. Thankfully, the blood has already stopped seeping from Jesse's wound. The skin has pulled tight, torn edges mending together like magic. I blink. Maybe I hadn't seen it clearly before. Maybe the damage wasn't as bad as I'd thought.

"We should go." He pulls me to my feet. I manage to stand without swaying. "Can you walk?"

"I…Yes." And I can. I can walk. I can talk. Aside from being on the verge of a mental breakdown, I'm faring better than I should be. It's almost like when I was a kid, when for a few short weeks I didn't need insulin shots at all. My body responded to the new medication so positively, my doctors dared to think that my dad and the other chemists at North Corp might have found the cure for juvenile diabetes.

But then my body turned on me. First my immune system, then my mind. Rachel came to me not long after, and life was never the same.

"Come on, it's not far and we should get inside." Jesse pulls me forward. I follow, rushing faster when the sirens get louder, feeling as if I'm somehow responsible for the crash that killed my friend and classmates.

And who knows…maybe I am. Jesse limps along beside me, the leg Rachel crushed clearly causing him pain, bringing home the fact, with every step he takes, that my "imaginary friend" has hurt another person.

Imaginary friend. My parents and the doctors and the nurses with their pitying faces—all of them were wrong.

Rachel isn't imaginary, and she's no one's friend.

Jesse

Just past another overpass—this one black with age and covered with creeping vines—we climb up the side of the ravine. We hurry past rotting trash, shattered beer bottles, the remains of a camp fire, and a couple of used condoms that would make me uncomfortable at any other time. Nasty rubbers aren't the kind of thing you want to step over when you're holding a girl's hand.

But I'm beyond any weird feelings about Dani's fingers being wrapped in mine. When we finally reach the street and she leans against me, I don't hesitate to wrap my arm around her shoulders. Sometime in the past half hour, being close to Dani has become natural, necessary. The world's flipped upside down and we're the only thing either of us has left to hold onto, the last defense against the monster trying to kill us.

Did you see it? Did you see a dragon in that tree? Did you?

The question slams around in my mind, begging to be asked, but I don't dare. Not yet. We have to get Dani something to eat or drink first. She seems to be doing okay, but the last thing I want is for her to pass out again.

I need her eyes open, helping me watch out for danger, assuring me I'm not completely out of my mind.

"There's nothing here," she whispers, scanning the deserted street with its rows of abandoned, concrete-block houses.

We're farther south than I guessed, but the bar I'm thinking about isn't far. Good thing. There isn't much else near this part of the freeway. Just a locked-up gas station with bars on the windows and those gray buildings that used to be part of a muffler factory, if you believe the faded black sign creaking in the wind. Whatever they used to be, they're empty now. Or filled with people as scary as the thing that's coming for us.

Visions of sharp claws and fangs dripping with blood flash behind my eyes. The memory of how close Dani and I came to being dead makes me shudder.

Okay, so no homeless man or crackhead could be that scary, but it's pointless to go looking for food in a drug den. And we need to call…someone. Trent worked the night shift last night and is probably sacked out snoring in the living room, and Traci slept somewhere else. She does that a lot after her "girls' nights," and I know for a fact she didn't take her cell phone. I saw it on the kitchen table next to the overflowing ashtray and the newspapers that never get taken to the curb. But even if she had her phone, she wouldn't appreciate a call to come pick my ass up at a bar when I'm supposed to be at school and out of her hair.

But maybe Dani has someone. A girl like her, she probably has a lot of someones.

"Come on, this way." I start across the street, sort of wishing there were cars to look out for. I don't like this place. It's too empty and isolated. It makes it even easier to believe that Dani and I are the only people left in a world gone crazy.

"Where are we going?" she asks.

"There's this biker bar a few blocks up," I say. "I've been there before with my foster dad. Some of the guys look scary, but they're cool. They'll let us in and give you something to eat or drink or whatever."

"Will it be open this early in the morning?"

"It's always open. The night shift guys go there when they get off, start drinking at five in the morning and go home and pass out after lunch. And they've got a pay phone, so…"

"Okay, sounds good," she says, surprising me.

I expected more resistance at the idea of going into a bar. Dani has good girl written all over her, from her shiny, streak-free hair to her almost makeup-free face, to her choice of school uniform, a combo so modest she might as well be a nun or something.

But her modest clothes can't hide the fact that she's built like a supermodel, tall and slim and graceful. If I didn't know she was a dancer, I'd still guess it. Just the way she walks down the street is like a dance; the way she sways into me as we hurry down the cracked sidewalk makes me feel like I'm dancing with her.

I've never danced in my life. Never. Not by myself, not with a girl, not even in my dreams. But for a second I wonder what it would be like to dance with Dani, to hold her close at one of those stupid school balls.

"I have to call my dad as soon as we get there. A lot of his friends work at the hospital. I bet he's heard about the wreck," she says, reminding me that she's out of my league. Way out. Her dad's a rich, important doctor and will probably be about as thrilled about his daughter hanging out with a foster kid with an arrest record as he will be about picking that daughter up at a sleazy bar.

Besides, I don't do dances, or relationships. Every time I've tried, it's been a pain in the ass. Girls are never satisfied with a physical connection, even if they're the only one you're getting physical with. They always want to paw around in your feelings, get their hands on your secrets. My feelings and secrets aren't anything I want to share.

For the first time since the accident, the man in the glasses with his fistful of money crosses my mind. He paid me to get Dani on that bus. That's definitely a secret I don't want Dani to know, but is there a chance it could be something more? What if the accident wasn't an accident? It doesn't seem very likely, but still…

Still…

"So he might actually answer my phone call today," Dani says. I glance down at her, study the perfect slopes and curves of her profile. She's the poster girl for the happy, All American life. I'm insane to think someone is trying to hurt her.

But I saw the fear in her, both before and after the wreck. That kind of fear doesn't come from a happy childhood full of sticky Popsicles and summers by the lake. And that guy was a creep. I should tell her about him, just in case. I should tell her now, confess my sin and get it over with.

"If not, I can call my stepmom. She'll come for sure," she says, fingers curling into my arm. "She always answers on the first ring."

It's already too late. I don't want her to know the truth. I don't want to lose those fingers.

"Your stepmom's the blonde who picks you up after school?"

She looks up at me. For the first time in the past half hour, her brown eyes are more curious than frightened. "Yeah. Her name's Penny. She's cool. She'll take us both to the hospital if you want. Unless you—"

"Maybe she could just drop me at my house. It's not far from the bar."

"You lost a lot of blood. And your leg could be broken or need stitches." She walks in silence for a moment, scanning the empty parking lots on both sides of the road as if on the lookout for snipers. She definitely saw something in that tree that has her spooked. Could it have been the Thing? Is there a chance someone else has *finally* seen it? "And you don't want to get an infection."

"Yeah…I guess." I pick up the pace as the bar comes into view. The *Open* sign is lit and half a dozen cars and about that many bikes are scattered outside the cinder-block building. Just the thought of all those people makes me feel better, even if the Thing has proved it doesn't give a damn if people are watching anymore.

"I really think you should go. Just let them check and make sure you're okay."

"I hate hospitals."

"Me too." She sighs, a tired sound, but doesn't falter in her swift steps. She actually seems to be getting better instead of worse. It's weird, since she said she needed something to eat or she'd get sick, but I'm not about to question her recovery. I'm just glad I'm not carrying her into the bar passed out and twitching like she was after the wreck. "I spent too many years in them when I was little. With the diabetes stuff."

"Me too." Maybe that's our connection, the reason Dani is like me. "Not diabetes. It was some kind of kid cancer or something. It went away after a year or so, but I was in the hospital for most of fourth grade."

"Really? But you seem so healthy."

"I am now."

"I'm not. I thought I was better, or under control, but…" She trails off as we cross the parking lot.

"It's okay. We'll get you juice or something. They have food, too," I say, though I have a feeling she isn't talking about her blood sugar.

We reach the heavy wooden door and I tug it open, holding it for her. She passes under my arm, nose wrinkling slightly at the sour smell of decades' old split beer, but she doesn't hesitate. She walks right up to the bar, claims a stool, and asks the bartender with the braided, gray beard for a Coke before turning to me with an expectant look.

"I'll just have a water." I nod to the man, grateful that it's too dark in here for him to see that Dani and I have blood and mud on our clothes.

He isn't the bartender I've met before, but he obviously doesn't care if there are underage kids in the bar. If we ordered a real drink it might be different, but maybe not. The group of guys nursing a pitcher of pale yellow beer in the crowded booth across the room—skinny kids with patchy facial hair thinner than mine was in ninth grade—can't all be twenty-one.

"Do you have any quarters?" Dani asks.

"No."

"That's okay. Penny will accept a collect call. I'll call her after I drink some of the Coke. She'll bring money to pay for whatever we get. So if you want something, it's no—"

"I don't want anything," I snap. I don't let people buy me things, not even at Christmas when Trent and Traci have their annual burst of holiday-inspired generosity. I don't want to owe anyone and I already owe Dani too much. Sure, I probably saved her life by pulling her from the bus, but what about the man in the tracksuit? I could have been responsible for Dani ending up in some pervert's basement for all I know. I should never have taken his money.

"Okay." She nods, a blank look on her face that I can tell is hiding some other emotion. "Sorry."

Before I can apologize for making *her* apologize, the bartender plunks down our Coke and water and asks if we want a breakfast menu. I shake my head and he disappears, clearly not interested in small talk. Dani reaches for her Coke and claims the straw, slipping it between her lips and sucking down half the drink without pausing for a breath.

"Good way to get a brain freeze," I say, then feel like an idiot. We both have bigger things to worry about than a brain freeze from drinking cold Coke too fast.

Dani proves it a second later. Her eyes grow round and her lips part in a silent "O" of terror. When she speaks, her voice is so soft I have to strain to hear. "Do you see her? Down at the end of the bar?" Her fingers dig into my arm. "No! Don't turn your head. Just look. Slowly. She's wearing a brown dress, sitting on the counter by the beer taps. Can you see her? The little girl?"

With a careful shift of my chin, I slide the end of the bar into my peripheral vision. I can see the beer taps now—Bud and Coors and something from Ireland that Trent likes for chasing whiskey—but the counter next to them is empty. There's nothing there. Nothing I can see anyway...

The suspicion hits me hard, equal parts excitement and fear. What if I'm not the only one? What if Dani didn't see a dragon in that tree, but something else? What if Dani is more like me than I ever imagined? What if she has her own—

"We have to get out of here." Dani jumps off her stool, grabs my arm, and pulls me toward the door. "Hurry!"

"Hey! You gotta pay for—" The bartender's shout is silenced by the shattering of glass as the liquor bottles stacked against the wall behind him fly into the air, hurling themselves across the room and smashing against the dark, wooden wall inches from Dani's head.

She screams and crouches down, covering her head with her hands as she makes a run for the door. I follow, dodging bottles of whiskey and gin and vodka, just barely making it out the door as something explodes near my shoulder.

"Run! She could follow us! Run!" Dani snatches my hand and takes off down the street. I have no choice but to follow.

There's no way I can abandon her now, even if I wanted to.

Five

Dani

I run north, back in the general direction of home, not knowing where else to go. No place is safe. I'll never be safe again. Rachel is so much stronger than she was when I was a kid. Back then, there was no way she could have thrown things across the room like that, especially not so soon after knocking that tree limb onto Jesse's legs.

I'd assumed the branch was rotten and about to fall anyway and that's how she was able to knock it down. But what if that isn't true? What if she's strong enough to rip giant trees apart with her bare hands? She just hurled dozens of bottles across the room with the speed and precision of a major league baseball player. She certainly wasn't able to do anything like that before. Spilling coffee, carrying a needle clenched in her fist, pushing buttons on the machines that kept me alive—in the old days, those were the worst of her tricks.

But not now. Not now. Not—

"Dani, slow down. You're going to hurt yourself," Jesse calls from behind me.

"I'm fine, we have to keep going," I shout over my shoulder, so grateful that he's followed me. It would be better for him if he ran in the opposite direction and never looked back, but I feel so much safer with him around. And it isn't because of his size or his strength or his bad-boy reputation. It's because he's different. Like me. I've never felt so close to someone so quickly, never imagined this morning that I would be craving Jesse's touch as much as I've been repelled by physical contact with almost every person I've ever met.

"If you don't slow down…" He groans, reminding me of his bloodied leg. "Seriously, Dani. I can't keep up much longer."

The words make me stumble in my haste to stop. I trip over my giant feet and would have gone sprawling if Jesse didn't snag me around the waist and pull me upright just in time. The warmth that spreads through my body in response to his touch is nearly as shocking as the fact that I've almost outrun one of Madisonville Prep's star athletes. Even with Jesse injured, that should have been impossible.

I'm a dancer and in better-than-decent shape, but I can't go as long or hard as the other girls in the corps de ballet. I have to take a rest after fifteen or twenty minutes of dancing, a fact that's made me worry about how realistic my dreams of becoming a Rockette really are. There's a chance I'll never have the stamina to dance for an hour or more without stopping.

But now…Coke-and-adrenaline high aside, there's no way I should have been able to run so fast for so long. We're far, far away from the bar, so far down the access road that the industrial wreckage has turned to patchy trees and I can just make out the pale blue top hat of the *Shimmer Shine Diner* sign at the south end of Madisonville.

We've run at least five miles. Maybe more. And how long has it been since the attack? Fifteen minutes? Twenty at most?

"This is impossible." I put my fingers to my throat, astonished by the slow, steady beating of my pulse. My heart rate has already returned to normal. I'm not even out of breath.

"So you don't usually run like an Olympic contender?"

"No. Never." I look up at him, wondering at the strange light in his eyes. He almost looks…happy. No, not happy…excited. Is it possible that he feels the same things I do, that thrill at finding a similar creature, that shiver of electricity whenever we touch?

His hand moves to my face, thumb brushing softly back and forth across my cheek. For a second, I think he might kiss me and my lips prickle. I've never kissed a boy before. I can't remember kissing anyone on the lips, not even my dad or mom. I'm sure I did when I was a baby, but not since I've been old enough to remember it.

Now, I'm suddenly desperate to know what it's like, to feel soft skin pressed against soft skin and Jesse's breath hot on my lips.

I press up onto my toes, relevé-ing, bringing my face nearly level with his.

"Your cheek is…"

"It's what?" I'm almost afraid to speak, afraid to breathe, to do anything that will stop the slow movement of his lips toward mine.

"It's soft…" His breath rushes out and his eyes dart to the side, as if he's embarrassed. "But that wasn't what I…" He pulls his hand away. "You had a cut, after the wreck. It was bleeding, but now it's gone."

"Really?"

He nods. "And you seem so much stronger. And faster."

"I'm way faster. I've never run like that. I'm not even out of breath, and a lot of my symptoms went away before I drank the Coke. And that wasn't nearly enough Coke. I'd usually need the whole thing and maybe some candy too and…I just…" I bite my lip, shocked by how easy it is to talk too much to Jesse. Even with Mina, I always watched what I said, figuring it's better to be silent than sound stupid.

Poor Mina. I can't believe she's gone. Her mother is going to cry her eyes out. Her little brothers are only four and six. They won't know what to do without "Mimi" to pick on. They call her Mimi. I've always thought it was so cute and was so envious of the "turds" she locked out of her room when I spent the night.

I squeeze my eyes shut for a second before opening them wide, focusing on the hint of stubble on Jesse's chin.

"But what does it mean? Why am I different all of a sudden?"

"I don't know. But my leg is healing a lot faster than I thought it would, and the cut on my side doesn't even sting anymore." He pulls me closer, into a hug I can tell he needs as much as I do. "I've been thinking while we ran. Do you think maybe this has something to do with the things we're seeing?"

"You saw her? You saw the little girl?" My heart leaps in my chest.

"No. I saw…a dragon."

"A dragon. Like from a fairy tale?" I ask, more curious than surprised. After all, didn't I know? Didn't I *know* he'd seen something?

"Yeah, but horrible. It was on the bus right after the accident. It attacked me. Or us. I'm not sure." He shakes his head. "I was running from it when the bus exploded. I used to see it all the time when I was a kid. It used to…hurt me."

Jesse swallows, the effort it takes to perform that simple action telling more than words ever could. The dragon didn't just hurt him, the dragon traumatized him, scarred him so badly he can't remember what it feels like to have a good night's sleep. I smooth my hands back and forth on his chest, hoping to offer some comfort, or at least let him know I understand. *Really* understand.

"But no one else could see it."

I nod. "That's exactly what it was like with me."

"The doctors and nurses thought I was crazy," he says, relief in his voice.

Doctors and nurses. A frightening suspicion grows inside me. The warmth rushes from my skin, leaving me cold down to the bone. "You said you were in the hospital when you were little. What hospital?"

"Baptist Memorial, the ninth floor, terminal wing. Guess they didn't have much hope for me."

My stomach cramps. "That's where I was. I was eight. You said you were…"

"Ten." Realization dawns in his eyes and his fingers dig a little tighter into my waist. "I'm seventeen now."

"I'm fifteen. I won't be sixteen until June."

Jesse shakes his head. "We were both there at the same time."

"And we both…" I don't finish the sentence. We both know what I was going to say. We both have imaginary "friends," creatures only we can see, that try to take our lives.

"But the little girl—"

"Rachel," I say, grateful for the chance to share her name with someone who believes in her. And more importantly, in me.

"Rachel went away, right?"

I nod. "It took a while, but by the time I left the hospital I didn't see her anymore. I haven't seen her in years. Not until today."

"After the accident."

"Right. What are you thinking?"

"I don't know," he says, taking my cold hand in his warm one. "But there has to be some kind of connection between the hospital and the things we see. It's too much of a coincidence."

"Maybe there was lead in the paint at the hospital? Or a gas leak when we were there or something?" I ask, reaching for any explanation, no matter how far-fetched. "Maybe it made us crazy?"

"Crazy doesn't make bruises on your ribs from wrestling a monster half the night. And crazy doesn't make trees fall or bottles fly across the room."

He's right. There is something...magical going on. No, magical's the wrong word. Magic makes me think of *The Nutcracker*, of enchanted Christmas trees and journeys into fairy kingdoms where flowers dance and snowflakes come to life. But there are also rats in the Nutcracker's world. Rats, rats, rats. I definitely smell one. Something pungent and wrong that summons a spark of hope all the same. If something at the hospital did this to me and Jesse, then there's a chance it can be undone. If we can find out the cause, maybe we can find the cure.

I've never dreamt there could be a cure, that there might be a chance I could put Rachel behind me and know she was never, ever coming back. The thought makes me smile. Jesse smiles back, the curve of his lips transforming him into something truly magnificent. My breath rushes out and I forget how to pull another back in.

When he glares, Jesse is the ultimate gorgeous bad

boy. But when he smiles, he is…breathtaking. "You should smile more often."

"Maybe I will." His smile glows even brighter before it suddenly fades, vanishing as if someone slapped it away. "Dani…I…I think I should…"

"Should what?"

"I…" He scowls and drops his gaze to the ground with a sigh. "I just want to help keep you safe."

I squeeze the hand still in mine. "Me too. I mean… you." I blush, and hope the cold air will explain the pink in my cheeks. "Maybe my dad can help us. He's a doctor. Well, a scientist really. He works at North Corp doing research, but he helped with my treatment at Baptist when I was little and he knows lots of people. If we talk to him together, he might actually listen."

Or not. More likely, he'll think the boy I've brought home is on drugs and I'm out of my mind again. But my father's sharp, disapproving eyes don't seem as scary right now. Not when I'm holding Jesse's hand and know—for the first time in my entire life, beyond any shadow of a doubt—that I'm not alone.

Jesse

For a rich girl, Dani lives pretty close to the wrong side of the tracks. Her house is less than a ten-minute walk from the seedy diner at the edge of town, and only half a dozen long blocks from my own home-sweet-slum. The difference is that her street is a private drive that curves up into the hills, away from the depressed area below, round and round, past a locked gate where Dani has to punch in an access code, and then up another hundred feet. At the top of the hill, the dense woods thin away, revealing...a castle.

No, not a castle, but the closest thing I've ever seen to one. The house is three stories in some places, four in others, with dark gingerbread-looking wood and glass everywhere. There's an octagon-shaped tower room on one side. On the other, the roof turns into a giant deck that pokes up through the trees. I catch sight of the edges of what look like deck chairs and suspect there might be a pool up there.

A *pool* on her *roof*. I am...I have no idea what to say.

"This is it." Dani squeezes my hand. She hasn't let me go, not even when she punched in the code to the gate.

It makes me stupidly happy. I can't remember the last time I felt like this. It hasn't been since I was a kid, and maybe not even then. I have a hard time remembering much about my life with my birth mom except for that last year, when she met Neil, and me and my little sister became even more of a pain in her ass than we were before. It was the year she taught us the real meaning of neglect.

"I know it's awful. I'm sorry," Dani says. I see the worried expression on her face and realize I've been scowling.

I make an effort to relax, to stop thinking about things that aren't worth thinking about anyway. "No, it's fine. It's nice."

"It's too much. It's actually Penny's house. She's got a lot of money."

"Is she a trust-fund baby or something?"

"No, she was a freelance linguistic specialist for the FBI." Dani leads me across the gray cobblestones toward the front door. "She speaks five or six languages and developed this software that helped the spies spy better. Or something. She doesn't really talk about it much. She quit after she and my dad got married because she wanted to have babies."

"You have brothers or sisters? Half-brothers and sisters?" I'm strangely tempted to tell her about my little sister, the one I haven't seen since I was eight.

When I went into the hospital, Jamie was sent to foster care and almost immediately adopted. She was only six, as tiny as a four-year-old and the cutest thing I'd ever seen. She always made me laugh. Every day, even at the end when I was trying to take care of her by myself and I lay awake at night scared of every thump in the wall, thinking robbers were trying to get in, not knowing I'd soon have much scarier things to fear than robbers. Jamie was the only thing that got me out of bed in the morning. I loved that kid.

But by the time I got out of the hospital and the Thing finally went away, she was eight. I told the social workers I didn't want to see her. I figured she had a new life somewhere and was better off without me.

"No brothers or sisters," Dani says. "Penny couldn't get pregnant."

"Oh. That sucks." I swallow the lump in my throat.

Why am I doing this to myself? Why am I letting myself

69

think about all those stupid memories that I'd be better off forgetting? It's something about Dani. She makes me feel so much…*softer*. Soft enough for things inside me to crumble and all the sadness to seep up through the cracks.

I drop her hand at the first step up to the house. Before I can decide whether letting her go makes the aching better or worse, there's a crash from inside and a woman screams.

Dani rushes for the door and throws it open. "Penny? Penny!" She pauses in the doorway, scanning an enormous open room filled with overstuffed couches and a fireplace big enough to roast a pig whole. But there's no one in sight and the house is suddenly quiet. "Penny! Where are you? Are you okay?"

"Dani?" The woman's cry comes from the far right, back in the recesses of a room we can't see. "Dani, don't come in the house!"

"Shut up." A man's voice now, filled with a hearty dose of nasty. "Shut your mouth, Penny, you—"

"Run, Dani! Don't come—" Penny's warning is cut off by the sharp smack of skin striking skin. Then there are heavy footsteps and the crack of a door being thrown open.

I run for the sound, fists itching. Whoever just hit Dani's stepmom is about to learn what it feels like to be on the receiving end of a little violence. *Violence.* Nothing like violence to banish all that oozing softness. I'm almost glad I have an excuse to kick someone's ass.

I race through an arched doorway into a kitchen bigger than my entire house, with a cooking area to my right and a table big enough to seat twelve to my left. A woman with blond hair huddles on the floor close to the table, the contents of a china cabinet shattered on the floor around her. Her hand is bleeding, but she's definitely going to live so I don't stop.

I run for the open door beyond the table. It leads out onto a deck even bigger than the one on the roof, so large that the man hasn't quite made it to the other side. I get a good look at his back and an even better look at his profile as he dashes down the stairs leading into the woods. I'm close enough that I could take him in the forest, maybe at the bottom of the stairs if I jump the railing.

But I don't run faster, I don't jump the railing. I freeze, heart slamming in my chest as I realize who I'm chasing.

It's the man from the soccer game. The one who gave me five hundred bucks to make sure Dani got on the bus.

Six

Dani

"Penny! What happened? Are you okay?" I hurry to her, shoving aside shards of broken china with my shoe, memories from the past four years rushing through me…Penny, when we first met, making Dad take us to my favorite restaurant instead of theirs to make the "getting to know you" dinner easier; Penny, two years later, at her and Dad's wedding, giving me my own ring during the ceremony, thanking me for the chance to join my family; Penny, that day in seventh grade when I started my period in science class, checking me out of school and taking me to a movie, helping me forget how embarrassed I'd been by the long walk to the nurse's office in my stained jeans.

Penny has always done nice things for me. She's always there when I need her, never expecting me to say "I love you" back, never asking for anything but that I let her love me in place of those babies she can't have, and Dad doesn't want to adopt.

And through it all, I've always assumed that I *didn't*

love her, that Penny was nothing but an irritating reminder that my own mother can't be bothered. But now, staring down at her, seeing her face puffy and red on one side where Vince hit her…

I realize that I love her. I really do.

Tears well up in my eyes as I take her arms and help her to her feet. I'm shaking more than she is, and as angry as I can remember. I want to find Vince and smash his face in. I want to watch Rachel hurl a hundred heavy bottles at his head.

Funny how the idea of Rachel hurting people isn't as horrifying if it's someone I think deserves it.

"I'm okay. I'm fine." Penny sniffs. I guide her into a chair at the kitchen table just seconds before Jesse appears at the back door.

"The guy got away. He ran into the woods." His face is so pale, his lips look almost red against his skin. He's obviously freaked out, but why shouldn't he be? I told him I was taking him to a safe place, and all I've delivered is more awful.

But why? Vince has always been a leech, but he's never hurt Penny. In fact, I'd always assumed one of the reasons she gives her older brother handouts is because he makes her feel loved in a way Dad can't, in that warm, laughing-over-shared-memories-from-your-childhood, family kind of way. When they talk on the phone she usually sounds happy. Unless he's asking for money, of course.

Is that what went wrong? Did Penny finally tell him "no," and a slap across the face was the result?

"Do you want me to call the police?" Jesse doesn't sound wild about the idea. "They might be able to find him in the woods or something."

"It's okay." I pat Penny awkwardly on the back, wishing I had more experience giving her comfort. She's still hunched over, clutching her hand, sobbing, and it's starting to scare me. "We know where he lives."

"You do?" Jesse's eyebrows shoot up and the fear in his eyes burns a little brighter. But it isn't fear for himself. It's for me. For me and my family. The realization makes my chest ache. He isn't at all what people at school think he is. He's a good person, maybe even a great one.

"He's my brother," Penny whispers, voice fragile. I crouch down beside her, laying what I hope is a reassuring hand on her knee. "You were right, Dani. I should never have given him money. I should have forgotten I had a brother."

What? I've never said anything to her about Vince. "Penny, I don't—"

"I found the letter this morning, while I was getting the laundry from your room." Penny and Dad can afford a housekeeper—two housekeepers—but Penny likes to clean the house and do our laundry. She says it makes her feel like she's taking care of her family. "I only read it because it had my name on the envelope. I thought you'd left it for me on purpose."

Oh no. The blackmail letter Mina and I wrote after rehearsal. I must have left it out on my desk instead of sticking it in the drawer like I'd thought.

"I'm sorry, Penny. I didn't mean any of that stuff. I wasn't going to give it to you, I just…I'm sorry. I know you were only trying to help."

"He's beyond help. He always has been. He's probably going to end up in jail again, even if I don't press charges for today." Penny sighs, but lifts her head, swiping the tears from her face with her good hand. "Someone hired him to break into your dad's private files."

"What?"

"Your dad's research. It seems it's pretty valuable to someone."

"But isn't he still working on that arthritis thing?" I ask, before turning to Jesse to explain. "My dad does research for new medicines. He's been working on a shot to help people with arthritis since I was in eighth grade."

Penny takes one of the carefully folded cloth napkins from the table and presses it to her bleeding arm. "I'm not sure what they're working on now, but Vince said someone gave him twenty thousand dollars to steal Phillip's hard drive. He went into your dad's office while I was getting him coffee. I heard him in there and went to see what he was doing…" She laughs, a bitter sound that makes me angrier. Penny is always so upbeat and positive—almost annoyingly so. How dare her jerk of a brother make her feel this way when all she's ever done is try to help him? "He offered me a few thousand dollars to keep my mouth shut and let him take it."

Jesse clears his throat. "I…I think I need a drink of water," he says. "If that's okay? I can just get it myself."

"No, no! I'll get you something." Penny jumps to her feet. "I should have offered. I'm so sorry, I haven't even introduced myself. I'm Penny, Dani's stepmom."

"Jesse," Jesse says, but his voice is still strange.

But then, after the morning we've had, and being dragged into the middle of my extended family drama, it's amazing he can speak at all. "It's my fault," I say. "I should have introduced everyone. I'll get the water, Penny. You sit." I move to the cabinet where we keep the glasses. "Do you want anything else? Orange juice or apple juice or a Coke or—"

"Water's fine. Thank you."

I flinch. He sounds angry. Great. So far I've done a fabulous job of making the first boy I've ever brought home comfortable. I concentrate on pulling down a glass and filling it with ice and water from the refrigerator door. I'm grateful when Penny speaks, reminding me I have bigger things to worry about than Vince's attack or Jesse's comfort.

"What are you guys doing home from school? Was the field trip cancelled?" Penny asks. "I heard there was bad weather coming in from Buffalo and there might be snowstorms. I was worried about the bus coming home on slick roads."

My stomach sinks and my arm shakes so badly I nearly drop the glass of water on the floor. I would have if Jesse hadn't appeared at my side and plucked it from my hand. His takes my other hand with his, as if he senses that I need a bit of borrowed strength to tell my stepmom that my best friend is dead.

I tell Penny what happened, doing my best to describe everything with a minimum of horror. Still, by the time I get to the explosion, she's out of her chair, wild-eyed and gasping.

"Oh my God!" Her napkin-wrapped hand presses against her thin chest. "Oh my God, you two could have died. What about everyone else on the bus? Are there any other survivors? Why did you walk all the way home? Why didn't you call me?"

"I—I just, I—"

"I think we were in shock or something," Jesse says, coming to my rescue. "We just started running and didn't even realize how far we'd gone until we were almost back in Madisonville."

"Oh my God. Of course, I can't even imagine…" Penny shakes her head, tears in her eyes. "I can't believe this. You poor kids. This is awful. And all your friends…" Thankfully she doesn't finish her sentence. If she had, I might have broken down and joined her sob fest.

After a few uncomfortable seconds, Penny sniffs her last sniff and stands up straighter, obviously making an effort to be strong. "Okay, first things first. You could be hurt. We need to get you both to the hospital. I'll get my purse." She heads out of the room, voice rising as she disappears in the direction of her and Dad's bedroom. "Get your stuff together, Dani. Food and shots. We don't know how long we'll be waiting. I'll try to call your dad on my cell. You two can call Jesse's parents from the landline and have them meet us at the Baptist emergency room. We'll need his insurance information and I'm sure his parents are worried sick if they've heard about the accident. Has it been on the news?"

"Um…I don't know." I have to shout to be heard.

I usually hate it when Penny starts a conversation and then leaves the room in the middle, expecting me to either follow her or yell loud enough to keep up my end from three rooms away. But I'm not angry now. I'm grateful that someone capable is taking charge. I make a silent promise not to give Penny attitude for trying to run my life ever again.

"I'm not calling anyone," Jesse whispers, setting his empty glass in the sink, making me realize how thirsty I am. I head for the fridge and grab a bottle of water and a juice for the road. "My foster parents don't even know I was on the field trip. Even if the wreck's been on the news, they won't be worried."

I knew Jesse was a foster kid, but hearing him say it makes the fact seem even sadder. Something in his tone makes it clear there's no Penny at his house worrying about how he's growing up.

"And there's no way I'm going to Baptist. Not after everything that's happened."

"I could ask Penny to take us to my normal pediatrician," I say. "If we can convince her we're not really hurt that badly, then—"

"You told her we were in a bus that flipped off a bridge

and exploded. There's no way she's going to be convinced it isn't serious enough for the emergency room."

I sigh. "You're right. I'm sorry. I should have explained things better."

"No, I wasn't…I didn't mean to…" He jabs a finger at the fruit bowl next to the sink. "Can I?"

"Of course. Please. Yeah." He grabs a banana and peels it from the wrong end, the part without the stalk attached.

It's a little thing, but I store it away in my Jesse file, excited that I've learned something new about him. The banana disappears in a few large bites and he reaches for an apple, shifting closer to where I stand as he washes it in the sink. Penny always washes the fruit before she puts it in the bowl, but I don't tell him. It's nice to watch him do something so…normal. It makes it easier to imagine a time when he and I might just be friends hanging out after school.

Or maybe more than friends…

"I just…" He turns off the water, but keeps staring into the sink. "I think I should leave."

"Why?" So much for friends. Or anything else.

"You'll be better off away from me." He dries his apple on his torn sweater as he backs away.

"How can you say that? I'd be dead without you. That tree limb was meant for me. It was Rachel who made it fall."

He shakes his head, still refusing to meet my eyes. "You don't understand."

"I understand better than anyone ever has, or ever will. We have to find out what happened to us. If we don't…" I let the words hang in the air. He knows what will happen if we don't. We'll die. "I don't want you to go. I'm...I've spent my whole life thinking I was the only one."

Jesse's blue eyes finally meet mine. "Me too."

I draw a slow breath, shocked that a simple look can make me feel so grounded and off balance at the same time. "Now it's different," I say. "Maybe together we can find out what happened, and how to make it stop."

"Dani! Did you call Jesse's parents?" Penny calls from the other room.

"Not yet," I yell back, holding Jesse's eyes, willing him to believe with me.

"Do you want me to call them, then? What's his last name?"

Jesse shakes his head again, faster this time. "I can't, Dani. I'm sorry. Not right now. Your stepmom seems cool. She'll take care of you." He sets the apple on the cabinet and turns away, heading back to the front door.

"But who's going to take care of *you*?" My voice is a whisper, but it's loud enough for him to hear. He stops and glances at me over his shoulder, but the surprise in his eyes swiftly morphs into terror. "Get down!"

I don't question his urgency. I fall to the floor so fast my knees slam into the tile. But it isn't my bruised knees that make me wince; it's the heat that burns inches above my head. It feels like someone's set off a blow torch in the middle of the kitchen.

"Leave her alone!" Jesse screams. His hands are under my armpits a second later, hauling me to my feet, practically throwing me into the other room. Behind us, the heat flares again. Strong hands shove at my shoulders. "Run, Dani! Get out the door, hurry!"

I run, arms pumping at my sides, giving the sprint to the door everything I've got. I don't pause to wonder what Penny is going to think about what she's just heard, or about me and Jesse racing out of the house without an explanation. I don't even ask Jesse what we're running from. Even if I can't see what's chasing us, I can guess what it is.

He mentioned a dragon, and dragons breathe fire.

I burst out into the cold day and race down the driveway. I hear Jesse slam the front door closed—a barrier that lasts less than a second before the dragon smashes into it, cracking the heavy wood. And then Jesse is beside me, urging me to go faster, faster, the fear in his voice enough to coax more speed from my burning muscles. We hit the sloping part of the drive and hurl ourselves down the hill, running so fast we couldn't stop if we tried.

We don't try. It's still behind us. It's through the door and chasing us down the hill, sending bursts of fire to lick at our heels, forcing us to run even faster. Faster. Faster.

By the time the gate comes into view, my arms are blurring in my peripheral vision, my joints loose and screaming for my muscles to clamp down and take the necessary actions to stop the forward motion before I ram face-first into the wrought iron.

"Don't stop! Don't stop! There's no time for the combination," Jesse screams. "We have to jump it."

Jump it? It's four feet tall—even at the lower parts on the sides—and topped with iron spikes. There's no way we'll clear it. We'll rip our guts out if we try. I slow the barest bit and another blast of fire hits the back of my legs, burning my calves through the thick fabric of my wrinkle-free khakis. I gasp and pour on the speed again, my heart slamming in my throat.

Jesse's right. We have to try to jump it. Better eviscerated than burned alive.

I think.

The seconds it takes to reach the gate tick by faster than any in memory. One moment I'm fifty feet away, the next, I'm airborne, leaping for the fence, arms grabbing iron and holding tight as my stomach muscles clench and my feet shoot up into the air.

The next thing I know, I'm upside down. *Upside down*—suspended in a handstand on top of the fence for a stomach-flipping second—before my feet continue the journey toward the ground. My back arches and terror zips from my toes to the roots of my hair as I realize I'm going to have to let go or have my back slammed into the gate. I have to *let go*, and spin through the air and hope my feet find the ground.

I force my flexed fingers to uncurl and, for a second, I fly.

And then I fall—fast and hard—gravity snatching me back to the earth a second too late. My heels hit first and then my tailbone, the impact sending a tooth-crunching shudder through my body. The pain is sudden and immediate. I cry out, but the sound has barely passed my lips before Jesse is beside me, pulling me to my feet, looping my arm around his shoulders, helping me limp the rest of the way down the hill.

He casts a furtive look over his shoulder. "It's gone. I think. But I don't want to quit moving."

"Me either," I pant. "I could feel the fire. Was it... your dragon?"

"Yeah, but it's never breathed fire before. I can't...I didn't know it could do that." His arm tightens around my waist, pulling me along while I struggle to keep my legs moving. My tailbone aches so badly my entire pelvis hurts. There's no way I could keep going without Jesse's help. "And it's never come in the daylight before, either. Did Rachel?"

"No. Never. And she never came so often. It was once a night, sometimes twice if I was having a really good day."

He glances down at me, lifts an eyebrow. "A good day?"

"If I was feeling good," I rush to clarify. "She always seemed stronger when I was stronger."

He grunts. "That's...I think that was true for me, too. I never really thought about it before, but the Thing was harder to fight after I got out of the hospital, when I was supposed to be well."

"That's probably important. We should make a list of things like that." The thought of writing a neat, ordered list licks down a few of my frazzled edges. "And I have to call Penny. She's going to be scared to death."

"Okay," he says, "but I don't think we should go back to your house. I'm thinking we should…"

"We should what?"

"I think we should go to Baptist, but not the emergency room. I think we should go back to where this started and see if we can find any clues."

The thought makes me shiver. I haven't been back to the children's floor since the day I was released. I never want to go back, never want to feel that unnaturally cold air or smell the sour sharpness of industrial cleaner and medicine mixed with chicken noodle soup ever again.

But he's right.

"All right." I nod. "After I call Penny and my dad, I'll—"

"I think we should go before you call them. Otherwise they're never going to let you out of their sight. We might not get another chance."

"But I have to call them—they'll be too worried. Besides, I need one of them to bring me some new clothes. We're both covered in blood."

"Yeah…it's weird that your stepmom didn't notice."

"What?"

"It's weird that she didn't notice there was blood on our clothes."

We both think on that for a silent moment as we cross the street and take a turn into a subdivision I've never been through before. It's filled with older houses, all exactly alike, narrow two-story wood structures with small windows and saggy porches on the left or right. First left, then right, then left, then right—all the same except for the varying degrees of neglect.

Penny never drives through here. She takes the long way to the highway. She says this part of town is too depressing. She can't stand for things to be out of order, allowed to get messy and broken.

So why didn't she notice the blood on my hands? On my pants?

"I think she was too upset about her brother. She wasn't herself," I say. "And it was kind of dark in the kitchen."

Jesse grunts again, a non-committal sound. He turns left at the next stop sign, steering us past a dingy white house where a big-jawed dog lurks on the porch. It rises to its feet and snarls as we walk by. An animal like that would normally scare me to death. But after being chased by a dragon, a tethered dog just doesn't hold the same fear factor. Still…this neighborhood isn't the best, and Jesse and I don't need any more trouble.

"There's a gas station down Reginald Street. It might have a phone," I say. "If we head back to the main road, we could—"

"I was thinking we could go to my house," he says. "Just for a few minutes. It's around the corner."

"Oh. Okay." He lives around the corner in this neighborhood, a place I'd be afraid to walk by myself in broad daylight. The realization numbs my lips, and I suddenly have no idea what to say. He's seen where I live, the obscene mansion on the hill. It seems even more obscene by comparison.

"Traci, my foster mom, isn't much taller than you are," he continues. "You can wear something of hers. I'll change too, and we can get some money and maybe a car if Traci's there. She lets me borrow hers sometimes. If I tell her we're just going to take it to the hospital and back she'll probably be cool."

"Okay, but I really have to call Penny and my dad. I—"

"What will you tell them?" He stops and turns to me, arm sliding from my waist, leaving me colder. But at least I don't hurt anymore. The ache in my tailbone has mysteriously vanished.

We're standing in front of a faded yellow house with an exposed concrete foundation that's cracked in some places and patched in others—as if someone started work on shoring things up but never bothered to finish or fill in the dirt they'd displaced. A mound of earth crouches in the front yard, sprouting tufts of yellowed grass and patches of snow. Around the base of the mini mountain, cracked flowerpots and rusted car parts fight for space in the yard. In the garage, more car parts fill up one side and a collection of white, little girl's furniture covered with peeling stickers sits on the other.

The place is even more depressing than the other houses on the street. It makes me hope it isn't Jesse's...until he opens the metal gate, erasing any doubt. I hesitate for half a second, but catch the gate below the rusted flower decoration before it slams closed. I hurry after him, careful not to trip on the junk littering the yard.

"How are you going to explain why we ran? From the bus and your house?" He pauses on the steps and fishes a key from the mouth of a ceramic frog. It's a strangely cute thing, at odds with the rest of the rundown yard and porch.

"I don't know."

"Well, you'd better think of something," he mumbles, pulling open the screen door and working the key into the lock. "Or they'll think I hurt you."

His words startle me. He's being ridiculous. He saved my life. "No one will think you hurt me. I won't let them."

"You're you and I'm me, and no one's seen us together before today," he says in a tired monotone. "They'll think the worst, no matter what you tell them."

He tugs on the door, propping it open with one foot while he stuffs the key in his back pocket. Behind him, I get my first glimpse of where he lives—a cramped place stuffed with too much furniture that smells of old grease and older smoke. I fight the urge to wrinkle my nose, very aware of his eyes on me.

"Come on, we should hurry," he says. "We don't know how long we have. I'll try and find the phone—I guess your parents will think even worse things about me if you don't call."

"Forget it." I slip past him into the house, ignoring the smell in the kitchen and the piles of dirty dishes by the sink. "I'll call them after we go to the hospital. I need some time to think about what to tell them, anyway." And how to explain that I might not be coming home for a while.

Rachel hurt Jesse. There's a chance she could hurt Penny and my dad, too. If I can't find some way to get her under control, I can't risk going home. Even if I have no money, no clean clothes, and will probably end up on the streets in the middle of a freezing New York winter. But better to freeze than be responsible for the deaths of people I love. Better to die alone than put anyone else at risk.

My throat gets tight and something heavy pushes at the back of my eyes. I swallow. I refuse to cry. That won't do anyone I care about any good, and I don't want to give Rachel the satisfaction. She's gone for now, but a part of me is certain she knows what's going on in my world, that she's aware of how close she is to driving me to the edge. I won't tumble over. Not now. Not ever, if I can help it.

I turn back to Jesse. "Are your parents home?"

"Foster parents." He shakes his head. "No. I guess Traci's still out, and Trent…" He shrugs. "I don't know where he is. It's better that they're not here. We can get in and out faster and get a cab to the hospital. I've got some money." He heads down the narrow hall leading out of the kitchen, his shoulders looming even larger in the cramped space. "The bedrooms are upstairs."

I follow him, trying to ignore the nervous sensation fluttering in my stomach. After everything that's happened, the fact that I'm following a boy into his bedroom for the first time shouldn't even register on my stress radar.

Just like I shouldn't have been chased by an invisible dragon and I shouldn't be feeling so good with my sugar unbalanced and I shouldn't have been able to flip over that gate like some kind of ninja assassin. "Shouldn't" isn't a word that's doing me a lot of good today.

So I don't waste time berating myself for the mix of nerves and excitement that pulse along my skin as I trail Jesse up the stairs. I simply acknowledge it and make my feet move, knowing that he's right. We don't have time to waste.

Seven

Jesse

"Okay, so we're both healing faster, running faster, feeling stronger. What else?" I ask, loud enough for Dani to hear me through the bathroom door. I stare at the lined paper in my lap and do my best *not* to think about the fact that she's taking her clothes off in there.

Just handing her the jeans and sweatshirt I pulled from Traci's drawers was weird. I've never picked out clothes for a girl before. It was a strangely…intimate thing. Combined with the fact that I can't seem to keep my hands off Dani for more than a few minutes and I'm amazed I can sit still right now.

But I do. I sit, unmoving and focused at the end of my bed with my notebook, writing down everything we know about what's happened to us. Know thy enemy. I can't remember where I heard that, but it's always stuck with me. Knowing when the Thing would come, knowing the ways it attacked and the tricks it used saved my life when I was little. Now the dragon has stepped up its game and I need to step up my knowledge or I won't last long. Neither of us will.

"What about the timing of the attacks?" Dani's voice is muffled, as if she's pulling something over her face. Up and over. Off. I imagine her sweater falling to the floor and her fingers moving to the buttons of the shirt underneath.

I squeeze my eyes shut and refuse to imagine what Dani will look like when her button-down shirt joins her sweater on the floor. Even if she seems to like me—maybe even more than like me, maybe even want me the same way I want her—I don't deserve to imagine things like that about her. She would hate me if she knew the truth, if she knew that I'm part of the reason her life is in danger.

There's no doubt about that now. But why had her uncle—or step-uncle or whatever he is—paid me to get her on the bus? Did he just want to make sure she was out of town so he'd be free to come raid her father's office and rough up her stepmom in private? Or is it something worse?

I can't throw the feeling that the bus crash wasn't an accident. I keep seeing the semi's headlights in my mind, the way they raced for the bus so fast, like a bullet aimed from a gun. It's probably stupid, but I add "research crash" to our to-do list anyway, right below visiting the children's ward.

The bathroom door cracks open. I look up, meeting Dani's eyes. They're brighter now, sparkling above the white sweatshirt I grabbed. "You look nice," I say, the words out of my mouth before I can stop them.

"Thanks." She studies the floor, her cheeks pinker than they were a second ago. It's probably the cold. The house is freezing. As usual. Heat is on the list of things Trent figures we can do without in the name of buying more cigarettes. "The jeans are a little short."

"Oh…I didn't see." All I see is that the jeans that are loose on my scrawny foster mom cling to Dani's every muscle and curve. She looks good in jeans. Very good.

"So what do you think? Is there any kind of pattern?" She perches beside me at the end of the bed, close, but not too close. I can tell that she's nervous. Being alone with me in a room where a bed is the main piece of furniture isn't something that's going unnoticed on her end. It isn't going unnoticed on my end, either. Not by a long shot. I have to fight to focus on our conversation.

"Well, the dragon showed up the first time after the crash and the more I think about it…" I pause, the image of sharp claws scratching against glass flashing through my head. "It seemed like it was trying to keep us in the bus. I know that sounds crazy, but—"

"No, it doesn't. I mean, they obviously want us both dead." Dani's brows pinch together. "So you think the dragon knew the bus was going to explode?"

I shrug. "I don't know. I don't know if it thinks like that."

"But Rachel does. And she dropped the branch while we were trying to get away from the bus and threw the bottles when I was drinking my Coke at the bar," Dani says. "I was feeling better anyway, but usually I would have needed that Coke to keep from passing out."

A strange thought enters my mind. "When the dragon showed up at your house, I was getting something to drink and eat."

Dani cocks her head. "And Penny was getting ready to take us to the hospital."

"It's almost like…"

"Like they don't want us to do anything that will help us survive," she says, eyebrows unpinching as her lips curve. "Why are you smiling?"

I shake my head and turn back to my notebook. "It's just nice that we're thinking the same thing."

"Yeah. It is." She scoots closer. I catch a whiff of her grassy shampoo and barely resist the urge to turn and sniff the top of her head. Instead, I clear my throat and watch her long fingers uncurl as she points to the bottom of my to-do list. "That's a good idea. We should find out more about the wreck."

The wreck. The bus. Her stepmom's creepy brother and his money.

I cover the list with my hand. "Yeah." I should tell her now, tell her why I'm so interested in finding out more about the wreck.

"Don't be embarrassed," Dani says. "I make lists all the time. I love lists."

"That's not surprising." I stare at the pale freckles dotting the bridge of her nose. I imagine what they will look like in the summer when the sun makes them stand out dark against her skin. I bet they'll be cute. I bet she's even prettier when she's tan. I can practically see her nose wrinkle as she jumps off the swimming dock near the lake.

With effort, I cut my fantasy short, knowing if I start thinking about Dani in a swimsuit I'll embarrass myself. This is pointless anyway. I'll never see Dani in the summer time. If we live through the winter, she'll end up hating me like every other girl I've ever tried to know.

"So you're saying I look like a compulsive, list-making kind of girl?" she asks, her face moving closer to mine.

"No, you..." My words fade away. Her lips are so close. She wants me to kiss her. Do I dare? I shouldn't. She doesn't know me—not the real me—and she wouldn't like me if she did. I have to tell her the truth. I have to—

"You're right," she says, moving closer, closer, until I forget how to breathe. "I am a list-maker, and a little compulsive. And I'm usually very shy. And I've only been on one date and...I've never kissed a boy."

"Never?" The confession rings true. I saw Dani walk down the aisle of the bus. Even something small like that made her a total mess, and she's known most of the Mad Prep kids her entire life. Still, it's hard to believe no one's ever touched her. Some guy, some time in fifteen years, should have stolen a kiss. She's too pretty, too nice and easy to be with, and...funny. Unexpectedly, Dani's funny, too. Like now. Here she is, making fun of herself, daring me to play along.

"If Rachel had killed me with that tree," she says, "I would have died without ever being kissed."

"You're not going to die."

"I hope not. But just in case, I…" She swallows and leans so close I can feel her breath on my skin. But I can tell she isn't going to come any closer. She wants *me* to kiss *her*, not the other way around.

My heart races and my tongue slips out to wet my lips. I can't remember ever being this nervous before a kiss. I've kissed a lot of girls. Most of them older and more experienced than Dani. College girls. Some even older. Full-grown women I've met at bars who liked the fact that I seem dangerous. Girls our age—especially the Madisonville Prep girls—are usually afraid of me. Maybe because I'm a foster kid nobody wants, maybe because I'm big for my age and don't try to control my temper the way I should. Maybe because they can tell that I've had more experience with the shitty side of life than they even want to imagine.

Whatever their reasons, I'm not someone they invite home for dinner at their mansions. Those girls think they're too good for me, and I know I'm not good enough for Dani.

"Please, you don't have to mean it." The tremor in her voice echoes in my chest.

"Oh, I'd mean it," I whisper, heart surging up to pulse in my throat, making it hard to speak.

"Then mean it," she whispers back.

I can't remember if she moved those last few inches or if I did. All I know is that seconds later we're stretched out on my bed, Dani beneath me, kissing me like the world is going to end. And maybe it is. At least for us. Maybe that's why my entire body comes alive when her tongue slips past my lips. Maybe that's why I ache all over when she holds me tight, twining her legs in mine. Maybe it's simply knowing that this might be our last kiss—as well as her first—that makes it the *best* kiss, but I doubt it.

It's Dani who makes it the best kiss. It's because she looks at me with eyes that see beyond the mean, the bulk, the bullshit. It's because she isn't afraid to hold my hand, to let me take care of her, to trust me with everything, even her life. No one has ever trusted me like that.

No one ever should.

I pull away and force myself to move my body a few inches from hers. "I can't. I'm sorry. It's not you. It's... I'm—"

I'm a liar. I took five hundred dollars from a man I didn't know to get you on that bus and I've spent half the day running for my life with you and didn't tell you the truth. You shouldn't trust me. You shouldn't care about me. You should find someone who can really help you and let me live or die on my own.

I would have said something like that. The words were on the tip of my tongue.

But just then, someone knocks at the front door downstairs.

"Hello? Mr. and Mrs. Jennings?" The voice is low, deep, official-sounding, like the Department of Human Services workers who used to come check on me when I was first placed with Trent and Traci.

Back then, my foster parents made more of an effort.

They needed the check they got every month a lot more than they need it now. Traci was barely twenty years old and so depressed she could barely get up most mornings let alone hold down a job. She was the one to suggest taking in a kid. She'd been in the foster system and knew you could make a little money if you were careful.

So she and Trent pulled it together and did enough to make the social workers happy. It didn't take much—a clean kitchen, turn the heat on, make sure I was always dressed appropriately for the weather. The men and women who showed up at the door dealt with horror every day. A boy with a few bruises and haunted eyes from nights spent fighting an "imaginary" monster wasn't at the top of their needs-protection list.

I haven't seen a social worker since I was in junior high. Whoever this official person is, it's probably someone Dani and I don't want to see. Not if we want to keep our freedom and have a chance to investigate what happened to us at Baptist on our own.

Another knock, this one hard enough to make Dani flinch and her eyes fly wide. "Should we answer the door?"

"No. Get your shoes on. There's another way out," I whisper.

Dani scoots off the bed and dives for her shoes while I throw our notebook, all the cash from my secret stash, and anything else I think might be useful into my gym bag. A can of nuts, a few smashed granola bars I was planning to throw away, the waterproof poncho I wear when I go running on rainy mornings, and a flashlight—never know when you might need a flashlight—go into the bag. It takes less than thirty seconds, but already the knock and the voice come again.

"Jesse Vance? If you're in there, you need to come on out, son."

My mouth twists. *Son.* I hate that word. I'm no one's "son," especially not this condescending asshole's.

"This is Agent Bullock," the man continues. "I'm with the FBI. I'm here to help you."

Dani's eyebrows shoot up as she silently mouths, "FBI?"

I shake my head, indicating I have no idea what the guy is talking about. But something in his voice makes me want to run in the other direction. Maybe it's just my natural response to an authority figure—I've been pulled into the police station often enough to develop a healthy hatred of cops—but I don't think so. There is something… *off* about this. I haven't done anything worthy of the FBI's attention and there's no way an FBI agent would be investigating the crash this quickly. A cop at the door, looking for kids whose bodies they haven't found in the wreckage, I would buy.

But the FBI? It doesn't make sense. Until it does, I'll be avoiding Agent Bullock.

I take Dani's hand and slip out the door of my room, heading toward the window at the end of the hall, the one that leads out onto the sagging roof. I'd sneaked out this way fifty times or more before I figured out that Traci and Trent didn't give a shit if I walked out the front door so long as they didn't get a call from the police to come pick me up in the middle of the night.

We're at the window—sliding it open—when Agent Bullock calls out again. His voice sounds even louder in the hall, making it seem like he's already in the house, calling from the bottom of the stairs. The hairs on my neck stand on end.

"Jesse, is Danielle Connor there with you?"

The hairs on my neck go from standing on end to jumping around screaming. Something is wrong. Why is this guy so sure I'm here? And how does he know that Dani's with me?

"Do you think Penny called them?" Dani hisses.

Hmm. Did her stepmom call them? Dani said that Penny used to work for the FBI so maybe she has some connections, but even that doesn't seem very likely. "Maybe, but how would they get here so fast? It's been less than an hour since we left your house."

Dani nods. "And Penny doesn't know your last name. We didn't tell her when she asked. So how would she be able to figure out where you live?"

"Miss Connor is diabetic." Agent Bullock's voice is underscored by footsteps crossing the front porch. Several sets of footsteps. He isn't alone. The red-alert signal in my head flashes brighter. "She's going to get very ill if she doesn't receive proper care. You need to come out and bring Miss Connor with you, or we will enter by force."

Dani's fingers dig into the sleeve of the clean sweater I

pulled on. "This feels wrong. I'm scared. I don't care who they say they are, I think we should go."

The addition of her gut instinct to mine is all I need. I hitch my bag higher on my shoulder, crawl out the window, and reach back to help her through. I point silently to the soft spot on the roof where it isn't safe to step. She nods and inches along beside me, keeping tight to the house until we reach the right side where an old VW bus stands rusting in the yard. Trent keeps saying he's going to get it up and running and he and Traci are going to drive it cross-country one summer. So far, that plan has gone as far as the back yard, but the van provides the perfect jumping-down place.

It's only a few feet from the roof of the house to the roof of the van, and then an easy belly-slide to the ground. The fence that circles the front yard doesn't wrap around the back. Our yard bleeds straight into Mrs. Crain's, who, according to Trent, hasn't been out of the house since 1979. She certainly never seems to notice me rushing by her windows on my way to the street. She won't notice now, either. We'll dash across her patchy grass, hustle down a block or two, and come out near the bus station where it will be easier to hide. We just have to get out of here before Agent Bullock sends someone to check the perimeter.

I step onto the van—wincing at the metal thunk that seems to echo louder than it ever did on the nights I went out alone—and offer Dani a hand. She jumps lightly down beside me, making a much softer thunk, and drops to her stomach without being told. She eases to the ground, and I'm about to follow when she hisses in pain.

"Stop," she warns, the urgency in her voice making me freeze. "There's something here. It cut me."

I look over my shoulder, stomach dropping when I see the slashed place in Dani's jeans and the blood pouring from the cut on her shin. I shift until I can see the ground by the van, the sick feeling in my gut getting worse when I spot the rusted circular saw and the strips of sheet metal on the ground. Trent must have actually been working on putting in that new bed he's threatened to get finished by springtime, and left his tools out. As usual.

And now Dani is bleeding. A lot. And there are FBI agents—or men pretending to be FBI agents—on my front porch.

We have to get out of here. Now. I inch to my left and hop down to the grass. "Come on, I'll carry you." I ignore the firm shake of her head and scoop her into my arms. It's better if she keeps her leg elevated until we get the bleeding to stop.

I hurry across the yard, making as little noise as I can, shushing Dani when she tells me to wait. We're through Mrs. Crain's yard and back on the street, moving as fast as I can while carrying another person, when Dani punches me in the chest hard enough to make me grunt.

"I said, you can put me down now," she says, face flushed red. "So put me down."

"But your leg. It's better if—"

"My leg is fine." She points to her shin, where the

bleeding has stopped and the skin smoothed as if there was never a cut there to begin with. If I hadn't seen it a few minutes ago—seen how deep and nasty it was—I wouldn't believe she'd been hurt. My arms relax, trembling, as I set her on her feet.

This is crazy. This is science fiction shit. This is…very, scary weird.

"Yeah," she says, as if I'd said the words out loud. "I'm calling my dad. I won't tell him where we are, but like I said, maybe he'll know…something."

And maybe he will. I actually hope he will. It would be good to have someone say that what's happening to us is normal…even if I know it isn't.

Eight

Dani

The phone booth at the bus station smells like pee and the receiver smells even worse—like someone rubbed it into their long-unwashed armpit. I hold it as far from my face as I can and still hear the receptionist at North Corp asking me "which extension?"

"Dr. Connor's office, please." I wait while she promises to transfer me and the cheesy company-promo message begins to play. I would usually zone out during this part, but today I focus on the rich, female voice promising that "the work of today will be the hope of tomorrow," and that "donations to North Corp are appreciated and go toward building a better, healthier future for all people, regardless of race, color, or creed."

Anything to get my mind off the fact that Jesse is shoved into the phone booth with me, his chest only inches from my face. His eyes scan the area outside for trouble. His lips press tight together, as if he's trying to banish the memory of my kiss with pure pressure.

Kiss. I had my first kiss, and it was…amazing. Better than I ever imagined. It revolutionized my entire view of boy-girl relations. If *that's* what kissing feels like, no wonder Mina likes to do it so much.

Mina, my best friend who is dead, who won't kiss anyone ever again. The truth keeps coming back to knock me off my feet when I least expect it. How dare I be moping about the fact that Jesse wasn't affected by our kiss the same way I was? Mina is *dead*, crazy things are happening to my and Jesse's bodies, invisible creatures are trying to kill us, and I would swear I saw a flash of dark hair dart behind a tree in Jesse's backyard before I slid off the van…

I hold the droning receiver farther from my face. It always takes forever to transfer calls at North Corp. "I think Rachel was there. At your house."

"What? Where?"

"In your yard. I think she moved that saw so I'd cut myself. It's not as dramatic as the tree or the bottles, but that's the kind of thing she used to do when I was younger."

"Okay…" Jesse chews his lip. I turn to stare out the dirty glass, determined not to think about the way his lips felt on mine. "So you think she's getting weaker than she was this morning? Maybe she's used up her juice for today?"

"I don't know. Maybe. Or maybe she just thought something sneaky would be more effective." I sigh and tap my foot on the metal floor. "Or maybe I'm just *imagining* things, and she wasn't even there."

Jesse laughs beneath his breath. "Right. But it is kind of strange that we were at my house for over a half hour and neither of the things attacked."

He's right, but is it significant? "Maybe," I say. "And maybe not. Maybe they're both just tired." Does Rachel get tired? It used to seem like she did, but now the rules have all changed. There are so many things we don't know, things that are going to get us killed if we don't figure them out soon.

I clench the phone tighter, willing my dad to pick up on the other line.

"Or maybe they wanted us to stay there for some reason," Jesse says. "Maybe making out is bad for our health."

It's a joke, but I can tell he wishes he hadn't made it. Our eyes meet and the discomfort level in the phone booth shoots to amazing new highs. His lips part, as if he's trying to think of something comforting to say. Thankfully, my dad's voicemail picks up first. I don't want Jesse's comfort. I want him to like me the way I like him. Or at least not crack jokes that make me feel like a fool for letting my guard down.

"Hey Dad." I aim for an upbeat tone, but not too upbeat. "I know you're probably worried, but I'm okay. I'm with a friend and we're…okay. I just need to talk to you about something weird that's going on. A medical kind of weird. I'll try to call you again soon. If you could pick up when I do, that would be great."

"You'd think he'd be sitting by the phone." Jesse

watches me hang up the receiver and wipe my hand on my borrowed jeans. "Doesn't he have a cell you could try?"

"He has one, but I don't have the number," I say, embarrassed. "It's just for work emergencies. The company pays for it."

"What about family emergencies?" Jesse asks.

I lift one shoulder. "He doesn't like being tied to technology. Even for me and Penny." I follow Jesse out of the booth, grateful for the relative freshness of the fuel-scented air. We step up on the curb, close enough to the crowd of people waiting for the New York City bus that we seem to be one of them. "One time, Penny had to go the hospital for emergency appendix surgery. Dad was out for a bike ride and stopped at a different coffee shop than usual after. I couldn't find him for hours. By the time he came home and saw the note I'd left, Penny's surgery was over. Even *that* didn't make him give me his cell number."

I sigh, angry at my stupid father and his stupid beliefs that seem like another excuse not to be there for us. Penny insists that Dad loves us more than he loves anyone, but what does that even mean? How is that comforting when, as far as I can tell, Dad has no use for people? As long as he has his work and his morning bike ride, he's complete. Despite the fact that he pretty much devoted his life to helping me get better when I was little, sometimes it feels like Penny and I are just another concession to perceived normalcy. Like the expensive suits he wears because all the other doctors do, even though he couldn't care less about fashion. He has a wife and a daughter because it's expected, not necessary or important to him.

My jaw gets tight. "My dad's kind of a jerk," I say, surprised at how good it feels to say the words out loud.

Jesse shrugs. "At least he didn't lock you in a closet when you were little so he could go out and party with his friends."

The way he says the words make it clear they aren't hypothetical.

God. I can't imagine any of my parents doing something like that. It's terrible, and makes my whining about my dad not answering his phone seem completely stupid. "I'm sorry." I want to take his hand, but I don't dare. Things are still awkward between us.

"It's not your fault." He shrugs again, but it's stiff, uncomfortable. "It was my mom's fault."

"Do you ever see her now?"

"No. She wasn't there the day the child protection people came to pick me and my sister Jamie up from the house. And she never came to visit me in the hospital."

My jaw drops. Even my mother—the queen of uninvolved—was always there for me when I was sick. Always. "She never...Never?"

"No." He stares at the ground, seemingly fascinated by the gray smudges of old gum at our feet. "I don't know if she ever found out what had happened, or if she even came back to Madisonville. She and her boyfriend went to Florida that summer. Maybe they stayed there."

"They left you alone? By yourself when you were only eight? With your sister?"

"My mom said she'd be back before school started, but Jamie and I were home alone for a long time. It was okay at first. I knew how to cook a few things and we had lots of cereal. But then the rent didn't get paid, and the landlord came around and found out we were alone…" His voice is calm, even. The hands that fist and unfist at his sides are the only sign that he knows the story he's telling is awful. "He called protective services. They took me and Jamie to the hospital because we were underweight and not as clean as we should be. That's when they found the cancer or whatever it was. They checked me in and took Jamie…somewhere else. To an orphanage or something, I guess."

My hand slips into his. Who cares about awkward? I can't fathom what it must be like for him, to carry all this misery around in addition to the memories of the hospital and his dragon. "I didn't know you had a sister."

"I don't anymore. She got adopted while I was in the hospital."

"You never tried to find her?"

"Why would she want me to find her?"

I hold his hand tighter, wishing I had the guts to hug him. "You're her brother."

"So what? She's better off without me."

My heart breaks for him, a split down the center that fills my chest with sad and happy at the same time. I suddenly wonder what it feels like to love someone, someone who isn't family or a friend, someone who is a mix of both.

"Jesse, I—"

"Hey, you two," a man's breathless voice sounds from behind us. Jesse and I spin around and I stumble off the curb. "I've been looking for you everywhere."

It's Vince, Penny's brother. His face is beaded with sweat and his thick wool jacket is dotted with sticks and shriveled brown leaves—testimony to his run through the woods in back of our house.

"Run, Dani." Jesse reaches for me, but Vince beats him to it. He snatches my arm so tight I cry out and he tugs me back onto the curb. A few people glance our direction, but quickly turn their dark eyes away. Most of the men and women on the bench have children in their laps, and I'm betting very few of them speak English. But surely they can tell something bad is going on over here.

"No," Vince says. "You two are done running. You need to come with me."

"I'm not going anywhere with you." I try to pull away, but his fingers bite into my skin hard enough to make me wince.

"Let her go," Jesse says, his expression hard and dangerous. I'd be scared half to death if I were the one that look was intended for.

But scary looks won't go far with Vince, not if someone is paying him to get something from my dad. He was raised by the same people who made Penny a genius, but he totally missed out on Penny's work ethic. He's a con man and a thief and he's been in prison more than once. He must have decided the quickest way to my dad's research is through me, but there's no way I'm going to let him kidnap me in broad daylight. If I make enough noise, maybe one of the people on the bench will come to the rescue, or maybe someone inside the enclosed ticket area will hear me and call the police.

I open my mouth to scream, but Vince speaks before I can make a sound.

"I paid you to get her on the bus, kid, not become her fucking bodyguard." Vince jerks me closer, but I barely feel the hand clutching my arm.

Paid Jesse? Vince paid Jesse? To get me on the bus?

I search Jesse's face, looking for confirmation that Vince is lying. But he won't look at me. He stares at Vince like I don't exist, like we weren't holding hands a second ago while he told me all about his awful childhood.

"I don't want your money," Jesse says.

"You snatched it up fast enough the other day."

Vince's words punch me in the gut, steal my breath away. Jesse isn't who I thought he was. This entire morning has been a lie. His kindness, his "help," that kiss…

"And there's more where that came from if you help me out," Vince adds.

"The bus crashed. It went off an overpass and exploded," Jesse says. "There's no way in—"

"You two look fine to me." Vince's flat gray eyes are still, complacent. I know he couldn't care less about me, but shouldn't he at least be a little shocked?

Unless…

"You knew there was going to be an accident." My skin crawls as Vince's gaze settles on my face. "Our friends are dead!"

Vince smiles. "But you're fine, and the people I work for don't seem surprised."

Vince is working for someone and Jesse is working for Vince and the accident might not have been an accident at all. Someone might have deliberately killed my friends and Jesse is part of it somehow.

Images and thoughts flash through my mind, sharp-edged pieces of a puzzle I'm not ready to touch. All I know is that I have to get away from Vince and Jesse. I was stupid to trust a boy I don't know, even if we do share a curse. Just because we have similar enemies doesn't mean Jesse and I are friends.

"Let me go!" I scream as loud as I can, making every head in the waiting area snap in my direction. Vince pulls me close and tries to pin his hand over my mouth, but I twist in his arms. "Help! Someone, help me!"

"Be quiet, you stupid—"

"Let her go!" Jesse reaches for me, but I kick his hand, connecting with enough force that his fingers crack.

He flinches away with a betrayed look that makes me want to kick him again. How dare he act like *I've* hurt *him*? He lied to me, tricked me, made me believe and hope and wish when there's no reason to feel anything but fear.

The more I think about what he's done, the angrier I

get. Rage burns across my skin, banishing the winter chill. I've always been the victim, the sick kid, the shy girl, never the fighter. But I suddenly can't understand why. Why haven't I ever fought back?

Sure, I kept Rachel from killing me when I was a kid—I played a good defense—but why didn't I ever turn the tables? Why didn't I set a trap, make a plan? Why didn't I steal the knife from my dinner tray, hide it under my pillow, and do my best to rip Rachel open the next time she came to "visit" me in the night? Why have my only thoughts today been to run and hide? Why am I calling for someone else to save me when I could at least *try* to save myself?

Before the thought has fully formed, I fist one hand and slam it up and over my shoulder, aiming in the general direction of Vince's face. I put everything I have into the motion. Still, I don't expect Vince to let me go so quickly. The absence of his arms catches me off guard and I stumble. Jesse tries to grab me, but I push him away, half-falling in my haste to avoid his big hands. I don't want him to touch me. I'd rather fall on my own than stand with his help.

"Ahh, shit!" Vince screams and clutches at his nose. Blood pours through his fingers, ribbons of crimson that are more shocking than horrifying. I'm amazed that I hit him hard enough to bloody his nose, but I'm not sorry.

"Leave my family alone, and that includes Penny. Don't ever hit her again," I shout, the words lifting me up, the high of standing up to someone for the first time in my life giving me the strength to turn and run without another glance at Jesse.

"Dani, wait! Dani!"

I hear him call for me again, but his voice only fuels my churning legs. I push faster and faster, until the wind whips through my hair and stings in my lungs. Until my face is so frozen I can barely feel the wet running down my cheeks. I pretend the tears are from the cold and run on, not daring to stop and think of what it means to be alone and hunted.

Nine

Jesse

"Get her back here!" Vince yells after me. "Get her back here or you're *both* going to regret it. There's no running from these people! They don't take no for an answer. They'll lock you up, kid."

I sprint after Dani, ignoring his threats. People who don't take no for an answer are *exactly* the type of people I will never regret running from. Especially people who arrange deadly bus crashes that almost kill me and threaten to lock me up and throw away the key.

But they didn't kill you in the crash. And they've got people looking for you and Dani, like they knew you were going to survive.

But how could they *know*? There are no givens when you knock a bus full of kids off a bridge. Science is one of the only classes at Madisonville Prep that I actually find interesting, but it doesn't seem like even the smartest scientist could predict how the weight in the bus would have been distributed, the exact velocity of the impact, what side of the bus would hit the ground first, who might or might not be wearing a seat belt and what crap would be flying around. Dani and I could have been killed by a DVD player to the head. There's no way anyone could have *known* that we'd be okay.

There's also no way Dani's leg could have healed so quickly, or the gash in my side vanish by the time we got back to my house. There's no way we should have been able to vault over the fence at Dani's house like Russian circus performers, or that her tiny fist should have broken Vince's nose. At least, not hitting him the way she did—over her shoulder without a chance to brace herself or put her weight behind the punch.

But all those things had happened, and Vince's nose *is* broken. I saw the unnatural angle of the bone and the beginning of the crazy swelling that always comes with a facial injury. Dani messed that man up, and she nearly broke my hand.

Despite the pain that pulses through my fingers as I run, making my joints ache, I'm kind of glad she kicked me. I'm glad she fought back and that she finally knows the truth, even if she did hear it from the worst possible source. The way she looked at me—so angry and betrayed and disappointed—cut me up inside. I've already called myself every word for "stupid" I can think of, but I still feel like a load has been lifted.

Too bad another couple tons of crap has taken its place.

Now there's no doubt that something very big and bad

is going down. Something that involves both Dani and me and people who are willing to kill a few dozen kids in the name of picking us out of the bus wreckage. That must have been their plan, to come get us after the crash. But that brings me back to how they knew we'd still be alive.

Maybe, just maybe, there's someone out there who knows about Dani and me? Who knows that we're getting stronger, tougher, almost indestructible? It seems impossible, but our new powers and our old enemies are the *only* things that Dani and I have in common.

Another hundred questions race through my mind as I run, but I have no clue how to answer them. Especially not alone. I need Dani's help. Together, we might be able to figure out what's going on before the people looking for us track us down and throw us in the back of a van. Apart, we'll be dead by imaginary friend or captured by crazy people by the end of the day. Right now, I'm not sure which would be worse.

There's no doubt in my mind that the people looking for us are monsters, and a part of me has always thought it would be better to be dead than to go back to being ruled by fear and pain. I made a secret promise to myself that if the Thing ever came back, I'd take the easy way out. I'd put Trent's shotgun in my mouth before I'd go back to fighting for my next breath every single night.

But now…I can't imagine giving up so easily. Something inside demands I fight. Not just for myself, but for Dani.

I can't quit thinking about the way she looked right

after we kissed—hair rumpled, lips puffy, her eyes soft and dark. Something in my chest squeezes. I don't want that to be our last kiss. I don't want the only girl who ever trusted me to think I'm one of the monsters.

I sprint faster, following Dani across a crowded parking lot, past the entrance of one of those discount stores where you have to show a special card to get inside, and on, farther and farther. Past another mini-mall and down a side street that leads to the Madisonville historic district and the downtown shops on the commons.

She's running fast, but not as fast as she could if she really tried. I can feel her holding back, conscious of the heads that turn as we dash by. I'm holding back, too. If I push hard enough to catch up with her, I'll be running like a freak, someone there's no way the people we're passing won't remember.

We're already attracting too much attention. It won't take anyone who's looking long to figure out where we've gone. I have to make Dani stop. I have to convince her that I'm sorry and we need to work together.

And that we need to find someplace to hide. The sooner, the better.

"Dani! Stop! Please!"

She casts a quick look over her shoulder, but doesn't slow. At the next street she cuts left, heading away from downtown, up a steep hill lined with vine-covered houses. There's nothing up this way except a dead-end street and a trail that leads over the cliffs and down into the gorge, an isolated place I don't think Dani would go alone. It makes me wonder where she's headed. Maybe she knows someone who lives on this street.

If she goes to a friend's house, there's no way they'll let me in. If it's someone from school, someone who knows me—or at least my shitty reputation—they'll probably call the police first and ask questions later. I'll have to leave, and then what will happen to Dani?

I'm positive the people looking for us know way more about us than we do about them. They probably know where Dani's friends live. They'll track her down at her safe place and find some way to take her. Maybe they'll pretend to be talent scouts from some reality show or long-lost family…or the FBI.

The FBI agents at my door.

I curse under my breath and put on a burst of speed. The street is quieter than any we've been on so far. No one is out in the crisp winter air, and a giant blow-up Santa waving in a yard across the street is the only thing that moves. I push faster. I have to risk being seen running like a mutant in the name of getting to Dani before it's too late. No way were those FBI agents real FBI. They're probably people like Vince, hired to bring me and Dani in to whoever is in charge. And if those people can afford to hire a small army to track us, we're in even bigger trouble than we imagined.

"Dani, stop." I'm close enough now that I don't have to yell, close enough that I can hear her sob beneath her breath before she digs deep and pours on her own blast of speed.

She's fast, but I'm faster. At the top of the hill, she veers off the street toward a house with a yard big enough to double as a football field. I tackle her, praying no one is looking out their window at this exact moment and getting ready to call the police. As we fall, I hold her tight and roll hard to my left, making sure I take the brunt of the fall.

Still, we hit hard enough that we roll across the grass. Once, twice, three times.

By the time we stop I'm on top, a position uncomfortably similar to the one we were in half an hour ago. In my bed. The thought makes me swallow and my grip loosen enough for her hands to slip through my fingers.

"Get off me!" she pants, fighting as I try to regain hold of her arms.

"Please, just let me explain." I barely avoid the fist she lets fly at my face. I grab her wrists, using only enough strength to keep her from hurting me. "I promise I'll let you go if you'll just listen for one minute. Please!"

"You're a liar!" Her arms twist and her knee jerks up, coming close enough to hitting its mark that my stomach cramps and flutters. Quickly, I pin her legs with mine, determined to be able to have kids by the time we leave this yard.

Not that I ever want to have kids…but still. Girls have no idea how bad that hurts, and that's when they're kneeing you in the nuts with a normal amount of strength, not some kind of superhuman mojo.

Dani is definitely channeling some intense energy. I'm sure I weigh close to a hundred pounds more than she does, but it isn't easy to keep her pinned. When she arches her back, she nearly lifts me off the ground—a fact that seems to shock her as much as it shocks me. She freezes, her eyes wide, limbs trembling.

"I'm not a liar," I say, taking advantage of her brief silence. "I swear to you, I had no idea that Vince was Vince or that he was working for anyone else or that they were going to wreck the bus. He was just some guy that showed up at my soccer game. I swear."

Her eyes narrow. "Some guy who gave you money to lie to me."

"No, I never lied, I—"

"You did. You're lying right now." She thrashes and I struggle to keep her from freeing herself and taking her lethal fists to my face.

"Dani, please!" I lean closer, willing her to look at me, to see that I would never hurt her. "All he asked me to do was make sure you were on the bus, and that I was, too. That's it."

She stops struggling, but I can tell she isn't convinced. I'm going to have to work a lot harder. I take a deep breath, forcing myself to speak from that place of truth inside me that I so rarely have reason to access. I've spent my entire life trying to hide that place, to hide my fear and my craziness and my weakness. But for some reason…with Dani…I know she won't think I'm weak.

"I thought he was just some weird old guy."

She rolls her eyes. "Well, great, I—"

"But as soon as I took the money, I knew I shouldn't have. I was…scared. I didn't want him to hurt you," I say, my throat tight, images of Vince's hands on Dani making me want to punch something. Preferably his face. "I promised myself that I would follow you around the city and make sure you were safe. That's why I signed up for that stupid dancing Santa show."

"It's not stupid," she whispers, a softness around her eyes. The tension eases slowly from her body. "The Rockettes are amazing athletes. And talented performers."

"Oh." I'm suddenly very aware of the way her body fits against mine. Now that we aren't fighting, it seems strange to stay here on the cold ground, but I don't make any move to get up. She feels…good. Really good. "I…I forgot you were a dancer."

"How did you even know I was a dancer?" she asks, but seems more curious than suspicious. "We've never said a word to each other before today."

"Because I've noticed you." My cheeks heat at the confession. Am I actually blushing? Is that even possible? Just this morning I would have said "no way in hell," but that was before Dani. "I knew your name before Vince told me who you were. I knew that you're in the honors society and a dancer, and that you always wear pants to school."

"You like skirts better?"

"I like…"

"Like what?" she asks in a husky voice that makes me shiver.

"I like pants. I like…you."

She lets out a breath. It eases from between her parted lips and feathers against mine. I lean even closer, so close that a shift of my head will bring our mouths together…if she'll let me.

Will she? I can't tell. I can't read her feelings in her eyes anymore. She's still shut off from me, hiding.

"You noticed all those things?" she asks.

"Yeah. I think you're very noticeable."

"I'm not noticeable." Dani's eyes drop to my chest. Her eyelashes are so long, impossibly long, and dark against her pale skin. I've never thought much about eyelashes before, but I think about them now. Dani's are beautiful, another piece of her I could stare at for hours. "I'm the least noticeable girl at Mad Prep. I look like a twelve-year-old boy."

I snort; I can't help it.

"Are you laughing at me?" Her eyes flicker back to mine.

I smile. "You don't look like a boy. Not even a little bit."

"I don't?" she asks, the way her tongue slips out between her lips making me think that she's as aware of me as I am of her.

"No." Her ribs press against my chest when she breathes, her legs shift beneath mine. "You don't feel like a boy either."

"No?" Her chin lifts. Only an inch now. An inch and we'll be kissing again. But do I dare?

"No. I liked kissing you."

"Then why did you stop?"

"Because I felt bad." I push her hair back from her face and trail my fingers down the soft skin at her neck, shocked by how amazing it feels when she shivers in response. I know how to make a girl feel good, but I've never known it could make me feel so good. But touching Dani, seeing her breath get faster and knowing it's because of me…it's as good as having her touch me. Maybe even better. "I knew I should tell you about the guy who gave me the money. I promise I was about to say something when those fake FBI guys knocked on the door."

She bites her lip and her breath comes out in a rush, and I know I've killed the mood. I won't be getting that second kiss. Not right now, anyway. I roll to the side as Dani pushes up on her elbows, telling myself that it's stupid to feel so disappointed. She doesn't seem to hate me anymore. I should be grateful.

"So, do you think they're the people Vince is working for?" She brushes dried grass from the back of her sweatshirt.

"I thought they were people *like* Vince. You know, people hired to look for us, but maybe…" I shrug, standing when she does. "I guess they could be the ones who hired him."

"Whether they are or not, I don't think this has anything to do with my dad's arthritis vaccine. I think Vince was lying to Penny."

"Me too. It has to have something to do with us. With what's different about us." I try to read what she thinks of that idea in her expression, but can't. She might not hate me, but she still isn't open and easy the way she was before. It makes me feel like shit. I promise myself that I won't stop working until Dani knows she can believe in me and that I will never lie to her ever again.

"With Rachel and the dragon, and getting stronger all of a sudden," I clarify. "I mean, it's the only thing the two of us have in common."

Just the mention of her tormentor's name makes Dani's eyes dart nervously around the lawn. "Where do you think they are? Why haven't they shown up for a while?"

"I don't know, but I don't think we should let our guard down. About them or anything else. We need to find a place to hide. And we should probably eat and drink something."

"We can go in here." Dani motions toward the big house. "It's Mina's house. I know where they hide their spare key and I've got the combination for the security system."

"But what if her parents—"

"Her mom and stepdad work and her brothers go to kindergarten and daycare."

I study the dark windows at the front of the house. "Okay, but we shouldn't stay long. I have a feeling the people looking for us know who your friends are."

Dani nods. "I thought the same thing. Vince probably pumped Penny for information. But I just…I didn't know where else to go after…" She sighs. "I'm just glad we're not on different sides."

"Me too. I promise I'll do everything I can to keep us both safe."

"I believe you," Dani says, easing something inside of me.

It isn't trust, but it's a start.

Ten

Jesse

Dani turns and hurries across the lawn. I follow, slowing my pace to match hers as we circle around the side of the house. Up close I can see that the paint job is peeling and a few of the shingles have slid off the roof. They lie where they've fallen on the ground, a crooked obstacle course covering the grass. It makes me feel better about where I live. Apparently even rich people can let their houses start to look like crap.

Dani pauses near concrete steps descending down into the ground, ending at a door I'm guessing leads to the basement. She pulls a copper key from one of the cracks between the stairs and continues around the house. "We'll use the back door. They let their housekeeper go about a year ago, and it doesn't look like anyone's home. But if they are, they're almost never in the kitchen. Mina's mom doesn't cook."

I nod, ignoring the anxious feeling in my stomach as Dani lets us in and punches a five-digit code into the panel on the wall. We aren't technically intruders—Dani is a friend of the family—but it feels like we're doing something we shouldn't. I guess Dani feels the same way because she doesn't waste any time. She goes straight to the sink and fills two glasses of water. She pushes mine across the island and lifts her own, pounding it down in four long gulps before pouring herself another.

Suddenly, I realize how thirsty I am. Insanely thirsty. I gulp my own drink and pass it back to Dani for a refill as my stomach growls, sending up a hunger alert. I look up to see Dani sliding my water and a can of nuts across the island. Another can of nuts follows, and then another.

"They're really into nuts." Dani pops some cashews into her mouth and flips on the television near the sink, punching the buttons to lower the volume and then turning to the local channel where the weirdly tan weatherman is talking about a chance of snow. "I want to see if there's anything about the crash on the news."

"Good idea." I grab a handful of almonds and reach for another before I've even started to chew. I'm starving, and not a normal, just-had-a-killer-soccer-practice starving. It's like I haven't eaten in days.

"I think we need to eat more," Dani says.

"I had food in my backpack, but... Shit." My backpack's gone. Screw the snacks; I had nearly a hundred dollars in there.

"What's wrong?"

"I lost my backpack. I guess I left it in the phone booth."

"It's okay. I can pack something before we go. Mina's

parents won't care if we take some granola bars." She chews for a moment, swallowing before she reaches for the peanuts. "I think whatever's happening to us is making us burn through calories faster. Superhuman speed probably takes a lot of energy."

"Yeah, I was thinking about that too." Superhuman. Mutant. I've thrown the words around in my head, but there hasn't really been time to stop and think about them. "It's like we're on extra-strength steroids or something."

"But even super steroids wouldn't explain why we're healing so fast."

"No…they wouldn't."

She bites her lip. "Do you think another drug could have something to do with it?"

"I don't take drugs," I say. "I have a beer once in a while with Trent or out at a bar or something, but they make us pee in a cup every month for sports."

"All I take is my insulin or a Tylenol if I'm sore from dance class." Her hand dips into the almonds. She has interesting fingers, long, thin spindles that seem like they'll break if you look at them too hard. But they won't. I've seen how strong she really is. "Maybe what's happening is a side effect of drugs they gave us at the hospital when we were kids. Do you think we could have been on the same medicine? Even though I had diabetes and you had something else?"

"I don't know what I was taking in the hospital. They didn't bother explaining what they were doing to me. They just did it. I guess because I didn't have a parent there to ask questions." I shrug, uncomfortable with the look on her face, that same pitying look she gave me when I told her about my mom. "But I don't see how something we took all those years ago would start messing with us now."

"What if it's like cancer or something, and it's coming out of remission?"

"Both of us at the same time? And suddenly the things after us are stronger and so are we?"

She sighs and shakes her head. "You're right. It doesn't make sense. I still think we should go to the hospital." She wipes her hands on her jeans. "At least it's a place to start, and we're old enough to request our own medical records."

"Okay, I'll—" I get quiet as one of the news anchors announces "an update on our breaking news story" and what's left of our school bus flashes on the television screen by the sink. Fire trucks surround the wreckage, hoses trained on flames that still burn high enough to touch the bridge above.

Dani turns up the volume and the sound surges as the anchor announces that "twenty-four teenagers were killed, and six more wounded by the deadly explosion. Police are still looking for two students, passengers on the bus, who fled the scene soon after the crash."

"Oh my God." Dani's hand flies to her mouth as our school pictures from last year appear side by side on the screen. I'm scowling and she's barely meeting the eye of the camera. We look…strange. Crazy. Maybe even dangerous.

"If you've seen Jesse Vance or Danielle Connor, please

call the police hotline at 662-9867. Any information on the students, or their whereabouts, is appreciated."

Dani runs a shaking hand through her hair. "Are they saying—do they think—"

"They're not saying anything yet." I push away from the counter, anger and fear rushing in my chest. "But it's pretty obvious they think we had something to do with the crash."

"No! That doesn't make any sense."

An awful idea gets going in my brain, making the nuts I swallowed stick in my throat. "Vince said we'd be sorry if we didn't come with him. He said that the people he worked for would get us locked up. I thought he meant locked in a cage or something, but what if he was talking about—"

"Blaming us for the crash? But we were in the bus, too. We weren't driving the truck that hit us. We could have been killed! How could they make it seem like we—"

"I don't know how they'd do it, but I bet they could. If you've got enough money, you can make just about anything happen. I bet it wouldn't be that hard to make us look guilty."

Dani's eyes grow unfocused. The glass in her hand hovers between her lips and the counter and when she speaks, her voice is distant, haunted. "That can't happen. I can't let Mina's family think I killed my best friend."

"We don't know that she's dead." There's not much doubt of it, but I'm willing to tell a lie in the name of wiping that terrified expression from Dani's face. "She might have made it out."

"She was in the middle of the bus. She's dead." Dani sets her glass down in the sink. When she looks back at me, her eyes are strong, focused. I can see the fight in her again and I'm glad. We're going to need every bit of fight in both of us to get out of this mess. "We'd better go," she says. "It's a long walk to the hospital."

"I think we should try to get there faster." I put my glass next to hers and follow her across the kitchen. "The place where my foster dad works is downtown. It's only a few blocks from here and they always have cars sitting around. His boss fixes up beaters when they're not busy. I know where he keeps the keys."

She pauses with her hand on the door and turns to look at me over her shoulder. "We're going to steal a car?"

"We're going to *borrow* a car," I say. "Unless you'd rather take the bus."

Her lips press together in silent acknowledgement of my grim joke. "No. A car would be good." She turns the knob and steps out the door.

I hesitate in the doorway. "Were you going to grab something else to eat before we go?"

"No," she says, her voice soft. "I'm not hungry anymore."

I let the door close. I'm not hungry anymore, either.

Dani

Fiorelli's tow yard is a lot bigger than I thought it would be. It takes up two whole blocks behind the flea market downtown and is surrounded by a fifteen-foot-high fence topped with coiled barbed wire. It's scary looking, but when Jesse tells me we're going to climb over, I don't hesitate. I just start up beside him, clinging to the chain link, barely able to feel the pinch of the metal against my frozen fingers. It's December in upstate New York and Jesse and I should be wearing coats and gloves, but I haven't noticed their absence until now. I'm not feeling the cold the way I normally would.

Maybe I'm going into shock. Maybe the insanity of the morning is finally getting to me. But then, *physically*, I keep feeling better and better. I can't remember a time when I've felt so strong.

My muscles aren't even shaking as I climb, and at the top—when it's time to ease through a narrow space between the coils—I slide through without hesitation. My heart doesn't speed a bit, at least not nearly as much as it did when Jesse and I were lying in the grass and he almost kissed me again.

I'd wanted him to, even though I'm not sure I trust him. How can I trust a boy who took money from Vince? But then…how can I not? There isn't anyone else who can hope to understand what's happening to me, and I don't want to be alone.

Besides, I can understand why he did it. I've seen his

house; I've heard enough to know he's probably never had enough money to get the things he needs, let alone the things he wants. Can I blame him for taking Vince up on the chance to make some easy cash?

"You okay?" Jesse asks, reaching out to steady me as I jump off the fence.

"Yeah, I'm good." My steady pulse picks up, and my skin clings to his warmth as he pulls his hand away from mine.

Trust him or not, I'm starting to crave his touch in a way I've never craved anything. It would be frightening if there weren't a hundred scarier things to think about. Like death and prison and creepy grown-ups who might have hired a bunch of creepier grown-ups to hunt me and Jesse down.

And kill people. Like my best friend.

The increasingly familiar fire in my chest flares to life once more. Anger—no, *rage*—swarms inside of me. I'm going to make sure whoever killed Mina and all those other people pays for what they did. No matter what.

Jesse does a quick scan of the lot before hurrying across the hard-packed dirt toward a clutch of cars in the far corner. "There's a blue Oldsmobile Mr. Fiorelli just got fixed up. Trent was talking about it the other day. He wants to give it a paint job and resell it to a friend of his. I think I can get it open and started without breaking into the shed to get the keys."

"Then what?" I ask, keeping my voice low as I trot behind him. "How are we going to get it out of the lot?"

"We drive out through the front gate," he says. "Mr. Fiorelli doesn't come in until one or two in the afternoon unless he has to. They do most of their towing at night. He's not in the office now or the light would be on." He motions to the small white building at the front of the lot. "We should be good as long as I'm as fast with a hot wire as I used to be."

"You used to steal cars?" I'm more shocked than I guess I should be. I'm starting to forget that Jesse is the bad boy from school. It's hard to reconcile his dangerous reputation with the boy I've known today, the one who looks at me like I'm something precious he needs to protect, the one who said he was sorry and that he's noticed me, even *liked* me.

"No, I taught myself how to do it on the cars in our yard the summer before I turned thirteen." There's embarrassment in his voice, and I feel bad for jumping to the wrong conclusion. "Summers were pretty lame around my house until I was old enough to get a job." He stops beside an old car. The hood covering is peeling in long strips from the roof and the door groans when Jesse pulls the handle. It opens with a stiff lurch. "All right. Finally. Some good luck." He sighs as he eases into the driver's seat. "If he left it open, the key might even be in here somewhere."

As Jesse leans deeper into the car, hunting beneath mats and inside faded compartments, I take another look at what we're stealing. It's definitely ancient, and not in the best shape, but it will blend in with the traffic around town. It bears the battle scars of an upstate winter, including several dents and rust that spreads like a nasty infection from the metal around the tires.

"Infection." I only realize I've said the word aloud when Jesse turns back to me with raised eyebrows. "I was just thinking…" My toes push inside my tennis shoes, lifting me up to relevé and back down again as my mind whirls faster than any dancer can spin. "What if this is some kind of infection?"

"Like a disease?"

"No, not a disease. Maybe infection is the wrong word. I just…I was thinking…" My breath rushes out, leaving a puff of cold that lingers in front of my lips before it fades away. "I was thinking that maybe this isn't happening because of medicine we took when we were kids. Maybe it's something we've taken recently."

Jesse sits up, long legs dangling out of the car onto the ground. "You think these people gave us something to make us crazy again?"

"We're not crazy."

"You know what I mean."

I do. I absolutely do. I pace to the rear of the car and back again. "Yeah, maybe they gave us something that made Rachel and your dragon come back, something that's also making us stronger, and—"

"Strong enough to survive a fall off a bridge?" Jesse shakes his head. "Assuming you're right, and there's a drug that could do that, how would they have given it to both of us? Slipped it into our food or something?"

I bite my lip. "I don't know. I could ask my dad. I need to call him again soon, anyway." The thought of calling my dad isn't nearly as comforting as it was an hour ago. The more Jesse and I learn, the more it seems like no one will be able to help us, not even the people who care about us the most. "I just saw the rust around the wheels, and—"

"The wheels!" Jesse rolls out of the car and kneels beside the back wheel, reaching questing fingers underneath. A second later one of his Jesse smiles curves the edges of his lips, making my heart skip a beat as he pulls the key from its hiding place. "Got it."

But before I can return the grin, his smile is blown away by a gust of surprisingly warm wind. Even before he opens his mouth, I know what's found us.

His dragon is here, ready for round two of barbecue tag.

"Get in the car! Now!"

I dive into the car, scramble across the gearshift, and bruise my knees as I fling myself into the passenger's seat. I turn back to search for Jesse, but he's already slamming the door shut behind him and shoving the key into the ignition. The engine sputters, struggling to come to life as something hits the left side of the car, making it rock onto the right wheels before crashing back down again. I grab a handle near the top of the window and a fist full of the slimy blue seat and hold on, not bothering with the seat belt. We might need to get out of the car fast. If Jesse can't get it started, we—

"Come on!" The engine grinds, but refuses to turn

over. Seconds later, something heavy lands on the hood, ripping a cry from Jesse's throat.

I can't see what he sees, but I know it's real. I can feel the jolt as the Thing makes impact, see the four dents in the metal where its feet have landed. No, not feet. *Claws.* I watch the scratch marks get deeper and longer as it digs into the hood. Then, suddenly, one set of tracks cuts off. Seconds later, the windshield pops as something big slams against it.

A crack slithers up the pane between Jesse and me, cutting us in two. A few more blows like that and his monster will be inside the car ripping us to shreds. Or maybe burning us alive, if it prefers its food cooked instead of raw. Acid rises in my throat, scalding away the scream trying to fight its way free. I am about to be killed by something I can't even see. For some reason even Rachel seems better than that. At least with Rachel—

I love you too, Dani. I spin to look over my shoulder and come face-to-face with Rachel's horror of a mouth stretching into a smile. Blood leaks down her chin onto her dress and her eyes flash meanly in skin the color of a bloated fish belly. *Let's be best friends forever!*

"Jesse, Rachel's in the car!" I shout as she lunges for me. She lifts the crowbar in her hand and brings it down inches from my head. I fall to the side, hand instinctively reaching for the door handle. I have to get out. I have to run, to—

Another blow hits the windshield and the air at my

neck is suddenly hot enough to make my skin pucker and sting. I can't go out. I can't stay in. I'm trapped, and Jesse and I are as good as dead.

Rachel swipes at me again. I jerk away, hitting the back of my skull on the rearview mirror as the iron sweeps past inches from my face. It slams into the passenger's side window, shattering the glass, giving the dragon a place to reach its claws inside.

I feel the cold air rush in and freeze, watching Rachel recover from the impact in slow motion, seeing her glossy hair spin as she turns back to me. If she doesn't get me, something else will, something that makes the car bounce as it jumps off the hood.

Bounce. Bounce. Grrr.

The engine shudders to life just as Rachel lifts the crowbar over her head. Jesse hits the gas and the car leaps forward, throwing her off balance. She tumbles into the tattered seats behind her as I fall into the passenger's side. I catch myself on the headrest, fisting one hand around the rod that leads down into the seat and bracing myself for a fight.

Jesse and I aren't going to die. I'm not going to give up, and running away isn't an option. It's time to fight back. Long *past* time.

Clinging to the seat, I dive into the back and grab for the tire iron in Rachel's hand. My fingers curl around the metal just inches above her tiny fist. For a second, we both hold tight. I stare down at her, shocked by how much bigger my fist is than hers. It's at least two times the size, maybe more, with strong muscles that stand out on the top and not a scrap of baby fat pudging my fingers. I might not be stronger, but I'm definitely bigger, more grown up. No matter how vicious she is, Rachel is still just a kid.

And I've outgrown her.

"Give that to me," I say, in my best big-person voice, the one I use when I'm helping Mina babysit and her brothers start climbing the shelves in the pantry. "Give it to me! Right now!"

Rachel's eyes narrow, her mouth opens in a silent, bloody scream, and then she does the unthinkable. She *lets go*. She gives me the tire iron, crosses her dimpled arms at her chest, and disappears. Poof. There one minute, vanished the next, a drawing on a dry-erase board smeared into nothingness. Not a fleck of color left behind.

I collapse into the front seat, clutching Rachel's discarded weapon in my hand, slowly becoming aware that the car is moving. Somehow, Jesse is managing to drive at a semi-reasonable speed through the narrow streets of downtown, though he's staring at me as much as at the road.

"What happened?" he asks, eyes flicking to the rear-view mirror.

"She listened. She gave it to me." My voice sounds hollow, shell-shocked. But what could be more shocking than this? Than discovering that maybe—just maybe—I've had the power to stop Rachel all along.

Eleven

Jesse

We park at the back of the cafeteria, wedging the car in behind some industrial-sized dumpsters and humming machines working overtime to heat the five-hundred-room hospital. Baptist Memorial isn't the biggest hospital around, but it's definitely one of the busiest. It's a teaching school and a research center and there are always people coming and going. The parking lot out front is jammed. It wouldn't have been easy finding a spot even if I'd tried.

I didn't bother. It isn't like I care if this car is towed. Probably better if it is. Then I can blame someone else for the dragon's damage. Maybe the hospital will even call Fiorelli's to lug the damn thing away.

Still, I manage to pull in far enough to hide everything but the bumper behind the dumpsters. We might need the car again, though as a getaway vehicle it has the major downside of taking *forever* to turn over.

The closeness of those last few seconds—when Dani was locked in a staring contest with an invisible girl and the dragon's bloody muzzle was inching in through the broken window—still makes me shiver. I don't want to tell Dani how close she came to having her throat ripped out. I don't want to think about it myself. I've never been so afraid. Almost getting killed myself is one thing; watching Dani almost get killed is something else.

Something much, much worse.

"I think we should try to find a disguise," she says as she squeezes out of the car.

We're so close to the dumpsters on one side, and to a stained concrete wall on the other, that there's barely room for either of us to open our door. It takes nearly a minute to slip through the narrow opening, shuffle down to the tail end of the car, and step out into the space where giant vents cough smoke into the air. We won't be getting back in very quickly, either.

I try to tell myself that it's okay and that the things hunting us won't be back for a while, but I don't really believe it. I'm losing what's left of my hope that we're going live through this day.

"I'm sure some of the people at the hospital have seen the news report with our pictures. It would be better if no one recognizes us," Dani continues, following me around the corner toward what looks like a delivery entrance for the cafeteria. It's deserted at the moment, but a planter sprouting cigarette butts promises that this concrete slab is a popular hangout. We should hurry.

"We're going to have to talk to someone anyway," I say. "When we ask for our records."

Dani hesitates on the last step, close enough to the butt planter that I can smell the tar and nicotine. "Yeah, I was thinking about that. Maybe we shouldn't ask. Maybe we should just…take them."

"Okay." I'm all about *not* interacting with anyone in this place. Just looking at the big red-brick building as we drove through the evergreens and up the tree-smothered drive made me want to smash something. I've never felt more small and helpless and out of control than I did in this place. Not even when Mom left Jamie and me. "But how will we know where to—"

"I remember where they keep the charts on the ninth floor," she says. "But I bet our records won't be there. They probably store the old records somewhere in the basement or something. But I'm sure they scan them into the hospital database first. I'm pretty good with computers. If I can get to one, I can probably find us."

"So we need disguises that will get us into a place with computers."

"Or just get us through the lower floors and up to the ninth floor. I know where everything is there." She swallows. "Rachel and I used to explore the hospital together, before she…before I knew what she really was." Her gaze meets mine, questions swimming in her eyes. "Was the dragon ever your friend?"

"Never."

"Not even in the very beginning?"

I shake my head, fighting the urge to grind my teeth. "No. The first time I saw it, it ripped all the needles out of

my arm. It took the nurses forever to stop the bleeding."
I close my eyes and see the nurses' angry, frustrated faces
again. "They thought I did it to myself. They strapped
my hands down for the rest of the night. When the Thing
came back, I had to fight it with my feet."

Dani's hand smoothes my back. "Don't be afraid," she
whispers. "We're going to find a way to stop this. I really,
really believe that now."

I nod. I don't want her to know that I seriously doubt
her story about Rachel obeying her command. The little
bitch probably just ran out of juice and is off wherever
the imaginary enemies go to rest up for their next attack.
I wish I could believe with Dani, but fear still tears at my
insides like dragon claws. I fought the Thing for years and
it never listened when I begged it to stop. It isn't going to
listen now, and it isn't going to stop until it has what it's
come for.

"Come on. We should get in and get out," I say. "I'm
sure those people are still looking for us, and they might
come here. A hospital's a good place for people who have
just lived through a wreck to end up."

"Right." She files silently in behind me as I crack the
door and step into what looks like a break room. Humming soft drink and chip machines sit against one wall
and scarred brown tables and chairs sit at odd angles in
each corner. Thankfully, there's no one around to observe
as we hustle across the scuffed tile to the double doors on
the other side.

Dani peeks through the door this time, turning to look

both ways before whispering, "There are some people working in the kitchen over to the right. But they look like they're cleaning up. We should be able to get across the room without them noticing. The doors to the cafeteria are almost straight across from here. I didn't see any uniforms or anything hanging around so I guess—"

"What about stairs?" I lean in, peering through the crack in the door. "If we can avoid the main floor and the elevators I don't think we'll need a disguise."

"What about *that* elevator?" Dani asks, pointing to the dull silver door on our far left. "Do you think it goes to the ninth floor?"

"If it's for delivering meal trays I bet it does." I take her hand, and a part of me relaxes for the first time since the latest attack. Touching her is...good. "Let's go."

We slip through the door and rush soundlessly to the elevator. Dani walks as fast on tiptoe as I do on flat feet. I bet she's a hell of a dancer. As I jam the red button by the door and take a quick glance over my shoulder to see if the people in the kitchen have noticed us, I silently promise to do whatever it takes to make sure she keeps dancing. Even if it means splitting up when we leave the hospital.

The Thing is bigger and stronger than ever and it's breathing fire, for God's sake. There's no way I can fight it and win. But if Dani *has* found some way to control Rachel, then maybe...maybe it would be best...

I can't even finish the thought.

The doors open with a much louder ding than I'd like, but it doesn't look like the sound carried. The guy mopping the brown stone at the far end of the kitchen doesn't turn around and the woman with her hand in a vat of coleslaw keeps kneading cabbage and mayo. Dani and I duck inside and around the corner, hiding behind the long panel of numbers. I hit the number nine and the doors rattle closed. In another second we're moving, gliding up to that little piece of hell I never wanted to set foot in again.

"I'm glad we're out of there. The smell was making me sick." Dani sounds about as excited to be returning to the Baptist children's ward as I am.

"Yeah. The food here was even worse than the stuff I'd burn for me and my sister at home."

"I can't even smell broth or Sprite without feeling things jabbing into the top of my hand," she says. "It always took the nurses forever to find a vein."

"Not me. I have good veins, I guess."

Dani pulls her lip in on the right side and bites down. Her thinking face. I'm starting to recognize it. It makes me want to kiss her. I probably already know her better than any of the girls I've been with. Dani makes me pay attention, makes me want to collect pieces of her like I used to collect hood ornaments off the cars in the neighborhood when I was twelve.

"You had good veins," she says.

"Yeah."

"Did you feel sick before? Before they took you to the hospital and found the cancer?"

I take a second, search my memory. "No. I didn't feel

great. Jamie and I had been living on dry cereal for a while at that point, but I didn't feel sick until I got here and they started the treatments."

"And the dragon came after." The elevator doors ding and we step out into a narrow hallway. A small, brown woman with black-marble eyes stands near the elevator separating the trash and the recycling. She glances up at us for a moment, but looks down almost immediately. She doesn't seem interested and I'm glad of it. The less attention we attract up here, the better.

I turn back to Dani as we walk, and keep talking. It's always better to act like you aren't doing anything wrong. Especially when you are. "The dragon came a few weeks later. After I'd been in the hospital for about a month."

"After you were feeling bad."

"Yeah."

"And the dragon tried to kill you right away."

"Yeah." I stop at the end of the hall and peer out into a larger hall with dimmed fluorescent lights humming overhead. The smell of medicine and sour sheets makes it hard to swallow. We're down one of the wings where the sickest kids are, the ones who sleep all day and moan all night. I used to be one of them. I wonder if Dani was in one of these rooms too? I wonder if our younger selves ever passed each other in the hall and had thoughts about each other. I can't remember a little girl with eyes like hers, but I've never been good at placing people on looks. I need to talk to them, touch them, form impressions that make them three-dimensional enough to remember.

"So what are you thinking?" I whisper.

"I don't know yet."

We start down the hall, footsteps nearly silent on the slick floor. The floors are nicer up here, polished and shiny, and the walls are covered with murals the kids work on every spring.

"An act of hope and renewal." That's what they called it when Dani and I were here. As if we didn't all know there wasn't hope for a lot of us.

Dani pauses by a painting of a field of flowers with a big, smiley sun rising over the mountains in the background. Her fingers float out to hover over a brown flower with a bright red center. "This was mine. I was so weak by then. I remember the brush felt like it weighed a ton."

I stare at the field, recognition slowly dawning. "This was the one I worked on too." I step back, scanning the blues and yellows and greens, finding an orange-and-purple-striped tiger lily with fat petals. "That's mine."

Dani smiles. "That's pretty good. Are you an artist?"

I snort. "That was the first and last time I ever painted anything. I only did it because we were getting ice cream after, and they said I couldn't have any unless I tried hard on the mural."

"That's a shame. Looks like you have potential," she says, her words making something inside me puff up the same way it does when I score a goal from halfway down the field. It's stupid, but I like the thought that I might be good at something other than sports, that Dani sees things in me no one else has bothered to look for.

She wanders down a little farther, to a framed picture on the wall by the mural. She leans in and sucks in a breath. "Is that you? It is, isn't it?"

I come to stand behind her, following her finger to the last row where a thin boy with improbably wide shoulders stands a head above the rest of the kids, even the ones who are obviously older. "Yeah. I was always really tall. It's weird because my sister was super short. But I'm not sure we have the same dad, so I guess…" I fall silent, searching the rows of pale, drawn faces and haunted eyes. Even the kids who are smiling look sad beneath the skin. They make me feel sad too, and when I finally find Dani I get even sadder.

"You." I point to the emaciated girl in the front, the one sitting cross-legged on the floor. Her bulging elbows are propped carefully on her knees, as if it hurts to touch the parts of herself together. The Tinker Bell on her T-shirt is smiling, but she isn't. She's biting at her lips, holding in a scream. Her face is skeletal, her cheeks hollow, and her bright brown eyes glitter with sickness.

Something catches in her throat when she sighs. "Yeah. I was really sick. Way before I came into the hospital. That's why they gave me the experimental treatment. They thought it was my only chance," she says. "But for a long time I just got sicker. It took months for me to get stronger." Her hand drifts up, lingering near the image of her old self. "When I was weak, Rachel was my friend. She would come play with me at night when I couldn't sleep.

It wasn't until the medicine started to work that she tried to kill me."

My arm finds its way around her narrow waist. I wish there was more of her to hold. Seeing how close she'd been to death makes me want to take her home and feed her some spicy sausage pasta, the stuff with the extra mozzarella and green onions that Traci and I go in on together if they have a deal on meat down at Bedford's. I buy the veggies, she buys the sausage, and I cook the hell out of some Italian food. I bet Dani would like it. I bet she'd like Traci, too. My foster mom can be cool when she wants to be. I wonder if life will ever be normal enough for me to invite Dani home, to make her the first girl I've ever introduced to my foster parents.

"But you don't look that sick here," Dani says, drawing my attention back to the picture. "Do you remember feeling sick?"

I shake my head, letting my lips brush against the top of her head, inhaling the scent of her hair. "No. Like I said, I only did the painting because they said we'd get ice cream and I think I ate a gallon of the chocolate. I almost never felt bad during the day. It was only in the afternoon after the treatment that I'd start to get sick to my stomach, and…"

"And what?"

"My muscles hurt a lot, and my joints. But I never…" I think back, a nagging feeling tugging at the back of my brain. "I was never weak or sick like most of the kids. I never lost my hair or anything. And I grew a lot while I was here. Almost five inches in a year and a half."

Dani turns in my arms, her hands pressing against my chest. She lifts her face and I read a new fear in her eyes. "You're probably going to think I'm crazy. But the more I think about this…and after everything you just said… what if you weren't sick?"

The idea startles me for a second. But only a second. That's all the time it takes for my brain to start sprinting down the path Dani has cleared. "If I wasn't sick."

"If you were just a kid with no parents and no family."

"And no one who was going to care if…"

If they used me, if they made me part of some kind of science experiment.

I think it, but Dani is the one who actually has the guts to say it out loud.

"If they used you to test a new diabetes treatment." Her hands fist my shirt. I can tell this conversation is making her sick. But then I guess for a girl like Dani, someone sheltered from the ugliest parts of the world, it must be pretty sickening to imagine a kid having his life stolen like that.

But if it turns out to be true, I won't be surprised. I'm way past being horrified by people. People are people, and a lot of the time they suck ass. This would just be another example in a long list of personal experience with the ass sucking. The only thing that shocks me is that I didn't think of the possibility sooner. Years sooner.

There's only one flaw in her logic.

"But how would that work?" I drop my voice as a nurse hustles down the hall behind us, rolling a machine with tubes spilling down from the top. She doesn't pay us much attention, either. Morning visiting hours just ended. Maybe she thinks we're relatives who haven't made it off the floor yet. "I know I didn't have diabetes."

She runs tight fingers through her hair. "I don't know, but when the scientists at my dad's lab are testing new drugs they like to give them to people who aren't sick, too. Just to see what kind of side effects they give normal people. North Corp is always advertising for healthy volunteers. They get a lot of college people and single moms…" She sighs. "But not many little kids. Not any, I don't think. That's why what my dad did was so controversial. Some people thought he was using me as a test subject. He had a lot riding on getting that diabetes drug onto the market. It could have made his career, maybe even won him a Nobel prize or something. Instead, it nearly killed me. And maybe…not just me."

"You mean your—"

"My dad is the one who developed the treatment. It was his drug," she says. "The first one he worked on for North Corp."

Twelve

Dani

I search his face, waiting for understanding to dawn, waiting for him to decide to hate me.

Even though we don't know anything for sure, a part of me is certain. I just *know* Dad did this. He was so determined to cure me. That's the whole reason he went to work for North Corp. They already had a medicine to treat juvenile diabetes in the works and promised that Dad could take over as head of the project. He would have done anything to help me get well.

Even put innocent kids through unnecessary pain and misery. He really doesn't care about other people. Penny says Dad's like a pack animal, willing to do whatever it takes to preserve his pack but missing a certain amount of "empathy for his fellow man."

Which is just another way of saying he doesn't give a crap about anyone who doesn't share his house or his genes. I don't know why I didn't think of this before. Why didn't this jump into my mind the second Jesse and I started talking about drugs we might have been given?

Because you don't want to believe Dad's really that bad. Because you're a dumb, trusting kid.

I wince. Harsh. But true.

"But if that's what happened, then…" I hesitate, not wanting to say another word, but knowing I have to. My father isn't picking up his phone, he isn't calling me back, and a horrible thought has already started to bleed into my mind. "What if my dad has something to do with what's happening to us now? What if he—"

"Hold on. You're letting yourself get way too far ahead," Jesse says. "We should look at our records first. We might not even have gotten the same treatment. I might really have had some kind of cancer. And even if your dad was part of something sketchy in the past, he isn't part of what's happening now. He would never hurt you. He wouldn't let people run our bus off the road, or pay Vince to steal his own hard drive."

I nod. He's right. I can't believe my dad would do any of those things. But still, if he's to blame for hurting Jesse, I don't know if I'll ever be able to forgive him. Or myself. I fight to take a deep breath, but the weight of my suspicions makes my shoulders heavy. "But what if… what if what happened to you is my fault?"

Instead of pulling away, Jesse leans closer. "It's not. Even if you're right. You're not your dad."

And then he kisses me. Soft and slow, his lips warm

against mine. I shock myself by giving in to the kiss, letting Jesse banish all the worry for a few heady seconds. His tongue slips between my lips, tasting vaguely of the almonds we stole from Mina's house and something else I can't quite place. Something salty and sweet and just…Jesse. Something that reaches past the shock of feeling another person's tongue against mine and makes the new intimacy seem natural. Perfect. So good I don't notice that we aren't alone until someone clears their throat.

Loudly.

I jump back so fast my head hits the mural. Jesse handles the interruption better. But then, he's probably had a lot more practice kissing—and getting caught kissing—than I have. He pulls his hands from my waist and crosses his arms over his chest, nodding a slightly cocky "what's up" as he turns to face the soft, bread-loafish-looking nurse standing a few feet away.

"Sorry," she says, a smile tugging at the wrinkled skin of her cheeks. "But visiting hours ended twenty minutes ago."

"Yeah, we know," Jesse says. "We're here to talk to somebody about volunteering with the kids."

Volunteering. It's a great excuse to roam around the floor every Thursday afternoon, but I don't know how it will help us today. We need to get to a computer *now*.

"Wonderful! The hospital can always use more volunteers. But we don't handle that here." She points toward the front desk. "You'll want to take the elevator to the second floor administration offices. Take a right when you—"

"We would have gone there," I say, trying to think as fast on my feet as Jesse. "But we wanted to make sure we'd get to work with the kids on this floor. We were both here when we were little. We're Danielle and Jesse?"

"Oh my. Danielle and Jesse." Her pale blue eyes move back and forth between us, not seeming to remember who we are.

But I remember her, even before she puts her arms around us both and hauls us in for a hug. Her coffee scent stabs at my nose, bringing memories of cold alcohol swabs and sticks in the arm. It's Coffee Nurse, the one who always took my last blood draw of the day. She's older and quite a bit wider, but her smile and smell are still the same.

She releases us after a moment, looking up at Jesse with a shine in her eyes. "And look how big and strong and healthy you both are." She sniffles. "This is why I stay here. Moments like this, when you know there's hope." She smiles again, this time a full-blown baring of her yellowed teeth. "Come on down to the break room. Let me get you two something to drink and we can talk about what you'd like to do with the kids. They're going to be so excited! It will be great for them to see that our kids can grow up so well."

My stomach starts to hurt as we follow her down the hall. I suddenly feel guilty for lying to her, and wish this *were* just a goodwill visit to sign up as volunteers. I want her hope to be well-founded. I want to believe that all the kids on this floor are precious to her and that their doctors are fighting for their lives. I want to believe Jesse and I will be coming back here to help out with arts and crafts and read stories and plan movie nights.

But I don't believe. And I know—even if I find a way to eliminate Rachel as a threat—that I'll never believe again.

Whoever did this to me and Jesse, whoever is hunting us, they're after us because of something that started here. In this place where we should have been safe. In this hospital, on this floor, where we slept and cried and prayed to be whole and our prayers were answered by monsters that came in the night.

And monsters with degrees in pediatric medicine.

I move closer to Jesse as we pass a pair of doctors conferring over some X-rays outside one of the private rooms. I'm glad when they don't turn to look our way.

The doctors have to be in on it. At least some of them.

You're being paranoid. This is crazy.

But I know I'm *not* being paranoid. That's the *really* crazy thing.

"I'll distract her," Jesse whispers as Coffee Nurse cuts behind the front desk, grabbing her ever-present mug before motioning for us to follow her back into the nurses' break room. "You make some excuse to leave and go find a computer. We can meet by the car in half an hour."

I nod, trying to figure out the best place to go. There are computers at the main desk and in the smaller offices at the end of the A and C wings—or at least there were back when Rachel and I made it our business to snoop around the floor after lights-out. The main desk is too public, and the A wing is for the kids who aren't super sick, so there will be more nurses wandering around checking up on them. I've just decided that the C wing is the best place to go when we enter the otherwise empty break room and see the bank of computers against the far wall.

Jesse shoots me a look over his shoulder. Without a word, I know the plan has changed. His new mission is to get Coffee Nurse out of here while I hit those computers.

Unfortunately, Rachel chooses that exact moment to make an appearance.

She materializes on one of the bar stools by the coffeepot and hot chocolate machine. She sits with her baby hands crossed in front of her. Her eyes are puffy and red. I freeze in the doorway, hands squeezing into fists, the terror she inspires a habit I'm not ready to break, though she isn't doing anything particularly threatening at the moment. In fact, she looks almost...bored.

No. Not bored, tired.

Her red slash of a mouth opens wide, her eyes wince shut, and her tiny jaw cracks softly. *Yawning.* Rachel just yawned. It's the most normal thing I've ever seen her do.

"You two want some hot chocolate?" the nurse asks. She walks past Rachel, close enough for Rachel's swinging foot to hit the leg of her scrubs. The nurse looks down and brushes a hand across the pink fabric, leaving no doubt she's felt Rachel even if she can't see her. She looks up at Jesse and then over to where I hover in the doorway, her smile wrinkling a bit when she sees I haven't followed them across the room.

"Are you too old for hot chocolate?" She reaches for the coffeepot and refills her mug. "Do you want some coffee instead? I just made a fresh pot. Or some juice? We've got orange and apple and cranberry in the fridge."

"I'll take some coffee," Jesse says, catching my eye, following my gaze to the counter where Rachel sits. She's propped her head in her hands and is shooting me a look that seems to ask why she's here. As if *I* am somehow responsible for…

As if *I* am responsible. Could it…Could I…

I take a cautious step forward. "Coffee sounds good," I say, even though it doesn't. I've never tried coffee. It reminds me too much of the hospital, of that last night when Rachel tossed this nurse's cup to the floor to create a distraction, clearing the way for me to chase her up the stairs to the roof.

It worked then. Maybe…

"Two coffees. Perfect." Coffee Nurse sets her mug on the counter and grabs two Styrofoam cups from a stack next to the pot. Now's my chance. Rachel's chance.

Knock it off the counter. Knock the mug onto the floor.

Rachel's eyes narrow before she slides her fingers along

the counter, closer to the mug, leaving no doubt she's heard my mental directive. But will she listen? Will she do it?

If she does…if she does what I've told her to do, twice in a row, then—

You're not my boss! Rachel lifts one of her fingers in an obscene gesture, and I fight a burst of laughter. There's just something funny about seeing a hand that size flipping the bird.

And there's something amazing about realizing I'm not afraid. For the first time since that night on the roof, I'm not afraid of Rachel.

Do it. I hold her gaze, letting her know I'm not going to back down. *Knock the mug off the counter.*

Rachel crosses her arms and wrinkles her nose, but one of her Mary Janes flashes out and sends the mug flying into the air. I watch it arc up, up, up with held breath. A breath I'm afraid to let out even when the ceramic smacks into the tile and shatters with a heavy thunk. Coffee leaps out in all directions, dancing weightlessly for a moment before it splatters to the ground and spills out, spreading like a suspicion confirmed.

By the time I glance back to gauge Rachel's reaction, she's gone. For once, I'm not happy to see her go. I want to look into her eyes and make sure she knows that she'll never have control over me again.

"Oh no!" Coffee Nurse slaps her ample thigh. "That's the third mug this month. I swear I'm going to start using Styrofoam like everyone else. The environment is just going to have to save itself."

Jesse grabs some paper towels from the counter. "You want me to—"

"Oh, no." She waves her hands in the air as she heads for the doorway I've just vacated. "I'll get the broom and the mop. You two go ahead and fix your coffees. I'll be right back."

She's barely stepped into the hall before I'm hurrying across the room to the bank of computers. I wiggle each mouse, rousing the screens to life, sighing in relief when I reach the third one. Whoever signed in last hasn't signed out of the hospital's back portal. Just a few clicks and I should be able to find my way to the records.

"Did you...did Rachel do that?" Jesse whispers, coming to stand next to me.

"She did. I told her to do it and she did. Then she went away, just like in the car."

"Wow. So...okay...you want me to lock the door?" Jesse's voice is careful, but his doubt still reaches out to wipe the smile from my face.

He doesn't believe me. But he will. As soon as we're out of here, I'm going to do whatever it takes to make him see that he has to believe me and he has to try. He *has* to. If he doesn't take control, the Thing is going to kill him. Or somebody else. Maybe even me, because I'm not going to leave him.

I can't ditch him to save myself. It's impossible. Even if I didn't suspect that my dad had something to do with making Jesse this way, I owe Jesse for saving my life half a dozen times this morning. And even more important than owing him, I care about him. A lot. A whole lot. Life without Jesse is starting to seem like not much of a life at all.

"Seriously, Dani. She could be back any—"

"The janitor closets are at the end of wings B and D." I type in my last name, then my first, and hit enter. One click, two, and now I just have to search for the right printer from the list. "It's going to take her at least ten minutes."

"Can you be finished in ten minutes? I—" He breaks off as the printer behind him roars to life, paper wheels rolling before the top page catches.

"That's my file," I say.

"That? Already printing?"

I smile again. I like his impressed tone a lot better than his disbelieving one. "Yeah. It's thirty pages, but that printer seems fast." I open up a new tab, type in his name, and hit enter. "And I'm betting yours will be shorter since…" I trail off, staring dumbly at the page that announces there are no results for my search. "This is weird."

"What?"

"It's not showing any record for you." I type his name in again, just in case I misspelled it the first time. "Nothing. Did you go by a different name when you were little?"

"No." He leans over my shoulder, staring down at the screen. "Let me try." He fingers find the home keys and he punches his name into the form with obvious concentration. He isn't much of a typist. His hands seem too big for a normal-sized keyboard. It makes me think of how much he said he'd grown while he was here, how he'd thrived despite his cancer diagnosis.

The idea creeps in slowly, like wisps of smoke. A smoke screen. Something to cover up the ugliness.

"There's nothing there." Jesse stands with a sharp, angry sound. "It's like someone erased me."

I click back, finding my own records and hitting the tab marked "medications." I scan the list, ordered by date, all the way back to the day I first checked into the hospital. I know most of the meds. There isn't anything strange or experimental there, nothing but the same scripts I've been taking on and off for years. "They didn't erase you," I say, throat going dry. "They erased the treatment. It's not on my chart, either."

"What the hell?" He drives a hand through his hair. "You were right. We had to be taking the same thing. That's why they erased me altogether. I wasn't taking anything else. They only gave me that one medication, in a drip through my IV every afternoon."

"Mine came through a drip, too." I sign out and hurry to grab the pages that have just finished spewing from the printer. They're useless to me now. I drop them into the shredder and listen to the razors buzz. "Let's go. I don't want to be here when she gets back. I don't think I can lie anymore. I'm not as good at it as my dad."

"Are you going to call him again?" Jesse asks, leading the way across the room.

"Yeah, I'll call him…eventually. But I was thinking

we could go to my family's cabin by Seneca Lake first. It's about an hour's drive and gets cold up there in the winter, but we could—"

"I don't think we should go anywhere your family's been before. We don't know how much Vince knows." Jesse pauses by the door and turns back to me with a pinched look on his face. I know right away that I'm not going to like whatever he has to say next. "And I think it would be better if we split up for a while. I could drop you at a hotel and then—"

I shake my head. "No. I won't leave you."

"You have to," he says, his tone taking on a hard, stubborn edge. "I don't want to hurt you."

"You would never hurt me."

"No, but the Thing in my head could kill you. It came pretty fucking close in the car."

The Thing in his head. In our heads. In our minds, our—

"I can't risk your life like that," he says, rushing on before whatever realization is tickling around between my ears can fully form. He takes my hand, squeezes my cold fingers. "I'm going to take you to a hotel a few towns away. Then I'll find someplace to hide and call you with—"

"Sir! Sir!" The woman's shout comes from just outside, near the front desk. "Sir! You have to sign in. And visiting hours are over. Sir, stop! You can't go down there."

"I'm looking for two missing children, ma'am," comes

a deep, syrupy voice I recognize immediately. "I have reason to believe they might be on this floor."

Jesse's grip on my hand turns deathly. He's recognized the voice, too.

Agent Bullock has found us.

Thirteen

Jesse

Dani and I press our backs against the wall just inside the break room door, holding our breath as Agent Bullock describes the two teenagers he's looking for. I close my eyes and cross my fingers, hoping the nurse at the front desk doesn't know we're back here. There wasn't anyone at the desk when we walked by. Maybe she'll send the agent off to roam the halls and Dani and I can make a run for the elevator.

"I'll send a message out to everyone on the floor," the nurse says. "But I can't let you search the rooms, especially with a gun. We have a lot of sick kids here and they—"

"I understand. I promise I won't disturb them," he says. "I believe the boy and girl I'm looking for will come with me willingly when they're found."

Right. That's why he has the gun.

A gun. My hand that's clutching Dani's starts to sweat. This guy could force us to go with him at gunpoint. My gut tells me our new super strength won't help us if it comes down to getting shot at close range. We're both healing crazy quick, but a bullet can kill in a split second, before there's any time to heal.

"Let me ask my supervisor," the nurse says. "What was your name again?"

"Agent Bullock. I'm with the FBI."

"Oh. I'm sorry." There's a clatter as the phone rattles back into its holder. "I didn't realize. I'm sure it will be fine for you to search the floor. If you'll just sign in here and let me get a copy of your I.D., I'll let the floor know you're coming through and to help you with anything you need."

"I appreciate that." There's a moment of silence and then large feet step away from the desk.

"And I just need your I.D.," the nurse repeats, a sliver of steel in her polite tone.

"I left my wallet and badge down in the car. I hope that won't be a problem."

The nurse makes a sound somewhere between a sigh and groan. "You know…I'm really not supposed to let anyone on the floor without getting a picture I.D. It's for the safety of our kids. Maybe you could run down and get it?"

"I understand. There are some real sickos out there," Agent Bullock says. "I think it's great you're so dedicated to protocol."

"Thank you, I—" There's sharp zap, followed by a guttural cry, and the unmistakable sound of a body crumpling onto the floor.

Dani sucks in an almost silent breath and grips my hand even tighter. I catch her eye and know she understands what happened, that Agent Bullock shot the woman asking for his I.D. Any doubt that the man means us serious harm vanishes as the nurse's thin moan fades to silence.

Dani trembles, a delicate tremor that echoes up my arm. I strain to track the sound of Bullock's footsteps, holding my breath as they draw closer, closer. He's behind the desk now. A few more steps and he'll be able to see us. I scan the room for the third or fourth time, looking for anything I can use as a weapon. But there's nothing, not even enough hot coffee left in the pot to do much damage.

I'll just have to use my hands and hope I'm strong enough and fast enough to put him down before he can shoot anyone else.

I drop Dani's hand and lift my fists. Beside me, Dani does the same. The sight of her anything-but-dangerous-looking hands balled up and ready to fight might have been sad if I didn't know she'd broken a man's nose with one of those fists earlier today.

Instead, seeing Dani ready to fight makes me feel stronger, safer. For the first time in my life I have someone I can count on. Dani is willing to risk her life for mine. The hugeness of it is too much to handle, but I know—if we make it out of here—that I'm going to *have* to handle it. I'll have to decide if I'm going to let her risk herself for me the way I'd risk myself for her, if the situation was reversed and I was the one gaining control of my demons.

Two steps, three. Agent Bullock walks closer, pauses for a moment, and then turns and walks away, shoes tapping against the tile as he circles the desk and heads down the hallway to the right. My hands shake as I drop them to my side, the force of my relief making my shoulder muscles twitch. I close my eyes and focus on his footsteps. He's definitely moving down the D wing, and moving fast. Which means we're going to move fast, too. In the opposite direction.

I grab Dani's hand and motion for her to follow me. She nods, holding tight as I step out into the hall and move quickly past where the front desk nurse lies crumpled on the floor. She's motionless except for her flickering eyelids. Her lashes blink a syncopated rhythm, Morse code warning me and Dani to run. She isn't dead. There's no bullet hole or any blood on the white tiles. If I had to guess, I'd say Agent Bullock probably hit her with some sort of Taser. Better than a gun, but a Taser can still be deadly.

Whether she's dead or alive, I don't plan to stop, but when Dani tugs her hand from mine I'm not surprised. I should have known she'd have to do something—that's who Dani is. A good person, who can't walk by a stranger in pain without trying to help. I wonder if her goodness will rub off on me if we're given more time together.

She grabs a cell phone sitting on the counter and presses it into the woman's hand. "Call for help when you can," she whispers. "I'll call and tell the hospital police what happened as soon as we get downstairs."

I don't wait for the nurse to nod before taking Dani's elbow and pulling her to her feet. We have to move. Now.

I cut around the desk, heading for the service elevator,

back down the hall we walked with Mercy. She's one of the few nurses whose name I actually remember. I always thought it was weird that the person in charge of sticking me with needles every morning and night was named Mercy. She was anything but merciful when it came to jabbing a vein. I can still feel the way her enthusiastic pricks stung at the back of my hand, made me bite back tears in an attempt to be tougher than the kid in the bed next to me. But I couldn't always pull it off. She was brutal. Despite her smiles and sympathetic looks, I kind of got the feeling she enjoyed her bloody work.

Maybe that's why I'm not surprised when we turn the corner and find her standing next to the flower mural, the photo from the year Dani and I helped decorate this hellhole clutched in her hands. She's talking to a tall man in a gray suit wearing sunglasses and a black ear piece, just like some cheesy Man in Black from one of Trent's action movies.

But he's the Man in Gray, come to take me and Dani away. Agent Bullock isn't alone. We just might be screwed.

"There they are!" The nurse jabs a pudgy finger in our direction.

Guess we know how the bad guys found us.

"This way!" Dani grabs my hand and pulls me back the way we came. I stumble after her, tripping over my feet in my haste to change directions. I'm never this clumsy during a game, but then the guys chasing me down the field don't have guns, either.

"Stop," the man shouts, his footsteps hurrying down the hall behind us. "Danielle, Jesse! Stop or I'll shoot."

Dani drops my hand and runs, sprinting for all she's worth back toward the D wing, faster and faster until her hair snaps around her face. I push hard behind her, kicking into superhero speed as we turn the corner and race toward the front desk. The man behind us yells again for us to stop, but doesn't make good on his threat to fire. Maybe we'll make it to the main elevator, maybe we'll—

Agent Bullock bursts from the doors leading to the D wing with what looks like a real gun, not some stun-gun alternative, clenched in his hand. I've never seen his face before, but I just *know* that this man with the sandy, gray-streaked hair and the fake'n'bake tan is the agent. I can imagine the way that smug mouth would curl up on the side when he called me "son."

He slows when he sees us and lifts his weapon. He's only a few feet from of the front desk. There's no way we'll make it to the elevator. We're trapped.

I skid to a stop. "Dani, wait! We—"

"This way!" She cuts to the right, into the laundry room. I duck in behind her just as the gun fires. I hear the bullet hit the wall and watch a piece of concrete crash to the floor. I slam the heavy wooden door closed and flip the lock without a second to spare. The smell of dirty sheets and bleach spins through my head, making me dizzy.

No doubt that's a real gun. And Agent Bullock is shooting to kill.

I back away from the door, clenching and unclenching my fists, fighting for a deep breath. Dani and I are as good as caught. A locked door will buy us a few minutes, but that's it. The nurse probably has a key to the room. If not, they'll just shoot the lock off and bust in. They'll be on top of us before we can—

"Come on." I spin to see Dani opening a small door in the wall. She lifts the metal hatch and hooks one leg up and into the hole beyond. A laundry shoot. "Give me a few seconds and then come down behind me."

She's getting ready to slide down a laundry shoot. Down *nine floors*, into a laundry room where there might or *might not* be anything to break her fall. I know I should tell her to get the hell out of there, that she's crazy and shouldn't risk her life, but I don't. I run, loop an arm around her waist, and haul her back into the room, silencing her protest with two words.

"Me first."

She wraps her arms around me, hugging me tight. The strength in her squeeze gives me hope that she'll survive the fall. "Be careful. Put your feet and hands out to the sides. It should slow you down."

Something slams into the door, and a male voice demands that we "Open the door! Right now!"

"Come right after me. Don't wait more than a second." I lift the door and wedge one leg and then the other inside, balancing on my tailbone. "If you fall on me it won't hurt. I'll be ready to catch you."

"I know you will." The trust in her voice makes my gut twist even before I turn to stare down the long, dark tunnel. Dani trusts me. I've won her back. We're going to get out of here in one piece. We just have to.

"See you soon." I push off, my heart jumping into my throat as I begin to fall.

I let myself slide for a few seconds, making sure I get a good head start, zipping down the metal tube like a kid on a very dangerous slide before spreading my legs and pressing my palms against the sides of the shoot. The friction is immediate and unbearable. My hands are on fire, melting, blazing, but I keep pushing until I slow down a little, then a little more. It helps that the tube doesn't go straight down. There's an incline of about twenty degrees, just enough to keep this tumble from being an out-and-out free fall.

Above me, I hear the shoot door slam closed again and then a shooshing sound and a rattle in the metal. Dani made it inside. The fire in my hands suddenly doesn't hurt quite as bad. She's on her way. I just have to make sure I'm ready to make good on my promise to catch her.

I pull my hands back into my body for a second and then push them back out. In and out, in and out, until I'm speeding toward the ground at a pace just short of insane.

It's also just short of fast enough.

The gun shot booms in the tight space. My ears pop and ring. The pain explodes in my shoulder a second later, making me scream as the bullet burrows into muscle. My left hand spasms and falls away from the side of the shoot. The shot must have zipped past Dani and found me. I'd be glad if I didn't know that first shot won't be the last. These people don't seem to care if they kill us, and for the next few seconds we might as well have red and white targets painted on the top of our heads.

Whatever's waiting at the end of this shoot—even if it's a concrete floor where Dani and I will both break our damned legs—it's better than a bullet in the brain. I give up trying to slow my slide and fall—faster, faster, faster, bones rattling and my heart oozing into my skull—until all of a sudden the fall is over.

I shoot out into a blindingly bright room, grunting as I land in a pile of stinking sheets. Vomit, blood, shit, sickness—it's all piled up underneath me, but I've never been so glad to roll over and press my face into a filthy pillow. My shoulder is on fire and I've had the wind knocked out of me, but I'm okay. Dani's going to be okay too.

She hits the sheets a second later with an *oof* and groans as she rolls into me, leaving a trail of red behind. My heart stops and begins the long, miserable journey back to my chest. Dani's bleeding. She's been shot; she could be dying.

"You okay?" she asks, voice tight, breathless.

She could be dying and she's asking if *I'm* okay.

I reach for her with my left hand, but a flash of heat and pain remind me I've got a bullet wedged into my shoulder. "I'm fine."

"You're not fine. They hit you, didn't they? They—"

"Don't worry about me. You're bleeding."

Her hands drift over her shoulder toward her back, but she winces and pulls away before touching whatever it is that hurts. "I think the bullet grazed me on the way by.

It doesn't matter. It doesn't hurt that bad. You're the one we've got to get to a doctor."

"No way." I scoot to the edge of the filthy pile, her words spurring me into motion. "We can't stay here."

"But you've been shot. You can't—"

"And the men who shot me are probably running for the elevator right now. We've got to go. Far. Fast." I hold out my good hand, helping her out of the tangle of sheets and onto the gray concrete floor.

She nods. "Okay. Come on. I was only down here once, but I think there's a back staircase. It comes out by the vents near where we parked."

She runs deeper into the laundry room, past towers of washers and dryers, into a storage area filled with industrial-sized containers of detergent and bleach. At the end of the metal shelves a tired, concrete staircase with a crack slithering up the side leads to a green metal door. Dani has probably just saved our lives. I recognize the door. We passed it on our way to the back entrance to the cafeteria. We're going to come out right next to the car.

We burst out into the cold, blinking in the sudden light. We're only a few feet from where we entered. The back of the hospital is as deserted as it was an hour ago, and the tail end of the dragon-trashed car still peeks out from behind dumpsters. As I follow Dani across the stained asphalt, I offer up a prayer that the engine will turn over on the first try. We aren't safe yet, but we're a hell of a lot closer than we were a few minutes ago. There's no way the fake FBI could have made it down to the ground floor yet. It feels okay to let my guard down for a second, to dig my fingers into my back pocket searching for the key.

I should have known better. I should have realized the car could be a trap. But I don't. Not until a man with wild brown hair down to his shoulders jumps from the space between the driver's side and the dumpster and throws himself at Dani. His arms wrap around her and she screams, a wounded sound that makes me want to smash his face in.

The key falls from my hand, tinkling onto the ground as I run for him, right fist lifting, pulling back behind my head. Dani shoves at his chest, giving me a perfect shot at his face. I go for it, thinking I'll smash his glasses and give us an advantage, but he ducks to the side, surprisingly fast for an old guy. Now that I'm closer I can see the gray streaking his hair, the bald spot near the back of his skull, and the wrinkles around his brown eyes.

Brown eyes that are…weirdly familiar.

For a split second I think I know him from some-where, but then Dani yells for me to stop. She fists my shirt and pulls me back as the man lifts his shaking hands into the air and I suddenly realize where I've seen those eyes before. They're Dani's eyes, the same melted choco-late brown.

I know he's her dad even before he turns to Dani and demands, in a perfect TV-sitcom-dad voice, "Give me your cell phone. Right now."

His daughter nearly died in a bus crash, and her blood

is smeared all over his right hand, and he's worried about taking away her *cell phone*?

"Right now, Danielle. I won't ask again." He holds out his hand, meeting my glare for a second before dismissing me with a flick of his eyes that says I'm not worth the effort it takes to focus.

I'm nothing, his daughter is his property, and he really doesn't give a shit about anything but himself. I see it all in a glance. Dani was right. Her dad is a total bastard.

I decide right then to punch him out if I have to.

I kind of hope I'll have to.

Fourteen

Dani

"Dad, you don't understand," I shout, ignoring the needles stinging through my left shoulder as I work my cell from my pocket. Dad's hug-attack ripped the healing skin apart, but I can already feel the wound getting better again. It's knitting up like a miracle, just like Jesse's did after I pulled the glass from his leg.

God, that seems like a hundred years ago. I feel like a different person than that girl who crouched in the cold sand shivering with fear. A stronger person, one who doesn't plan on letting her father get away with lying to her any more.

"Why are you here?" I demand. "What have you done, Dad?"

"Don't talk back to me, Danielle. We don't have time. Now give me the—"

"There are men trying to kill me and Jesse!" I fight to keep my volume down even though I want to scream, want to shove at his chest and demand he quit treating me like a child. Or a science experiment. I know he has something to do with all the bad things that are happening. His presence here confirms it. "They could be here any second. We don't have—"

"They *will* be here any second if you don't do what I tell you," he says, snatching the cell phone I've finally wiggled out of my pocket.

He turns and throws it into the dumpster behind him. My jaw drops. No matter how wealthy Penny is or how much he makes as one of the head honchos over at North Corp, Dad has always been frugal to the point of being cheap. And that phone cost over a hundred dollars.

"There's a tracking device inside," he says. "There was one in mine, too. I found it a few hours ago, right after two men ran me off the road on the way to work."

"What?" Someone tried to hurt my dad, maybe even kill him?

My anger drains away, leaving me so cold I can barely feel my fingers when Jesse wraps my hand up in his. "We should go," Jesse says. "If there really is a tracking device in that phone, throwing it in the trash two feet away isn't going to help us."

He makes a move toward the car, but Dad stops him with a hand on his chest. "My daughter's not going anywhere in that death trap. Both of you need to come with me."

"I don't know you." Jesse's chest puffs beneath Dad's hand. "And I don't trust you."

"I'm Dani's father," Dad says. "And I'm the only person who can help you."

"I think you've *helped* me enough already, sir." There's enough venom in Jesse's last word to send a roomful of adults into toxic shock. Usually that kind of disrespect would make my dad crazy angry.

Instead, his hand falls to his side, boneless and shaking. For the first time in my entire life, I see fear thin my dad's lips, tug at the edges of his eyes. He looks older, fragile. I'm suddenly aware of how small he is. This man who's always loomed so large in my mind barely comes up to Jesse's shoulder. He's nearly as thin as I am, with delicate wrists that Penny teases him about when they're shopping for dress shirts.

And he really is afraid. Because Jesse's called his bluff.

Actually, it's more like Jesse made a bluff of his own. One Dad falls for—hard and fast, a giant falling from the sky, crashing to the Earth at the bottom of the beanstalk.

"I'm so sorry," he says, his throat working. "We needed healthy children for the trial and I…I was just trying to save my daughter's life."

Oh no. Oh God. I can't…Even though I suspected, even though I told Jesse my theory that Dad could be a part of all this just fifteen minutes ago, I hadn't really believed it. Deep down, I'd still hoped my dad was one of the good guys and there was some other logical, less-than-horrific explanation for all this. But now he just keeps talking, slamming more nails into his coffin with every word.

"I never meant to hurt you or Dani or anyone else,"

he says. "We didn't know the medicine would have these kind of side effects. Real, documented examples of telekinesis were unheard of until the Dream Project. We never thought—"

"Get out of my way," Jesse says.

"No. Please, you don't—"

"Get in the car or get out of my way," Jesse repeats, shoving my dad back against the dumpster when he refuses to move. His hands fist in Dad's brown sweater, his knuckles turning white with the effort it takes to be gentle. He *is* being gentle. No matter how scared my dad looks, I know Jesse is holding back, being careful with this monster because he's mine.

My monster. Our monster.

My dad did this. He treated Jesse like a lab animal, put a healthy little kid in the hospital and stole his sanity, his sister, and God knows what else from the boy I love.

This is definitely what love feels like, this sensation of being ripped apart because of another person's pain.

I put a hand on Jesse's shoulder. He relaxes beneath my touch and releases my dad with a guilty look. I take his hand in both of mine and hold on, letting him know I don't blame him for losing his temper. I'm not mad at him. I love him, and I'm not going to let Dad—or anyone else—hurt him again.

"People are trying to kill your daughter." Jesse edges back toward the car. "We don't have time for you to say how sorry you are for ruining my life."

"Please." Tears rise in Dad's eyes, a wet sheen that makes

me sick. *Now* he's crying for us. Now that it's way too late for his tears to matter. "You can drive my car. I'll give you the keys. We'll never get there in that thing."

"Get where?" I ask, my voice as cold as my hands.

"There's a safe house about three and a half hours from here, near the Canadian border. More like a safe hotel, a compound-type situation," he stammers as Jesse snatches the keys from his hand. "The FBI is gathering all the kids who were part of the experiment there to keep them safe."

Everything he says seems like a joke. But it isn't. This is all for real. Deadly for real.

"The same FBI that put a bullet in my shoulder a few minutes ago?" Jesse asks. "Because if those are the guys who are supposed to be keeping us—"

"No. Those men are part of a terrorist group, they—"

"Come on. You can explain on the way out of here." Jesse backs away from the Oldsmobile, apparently having decided to trust my dad enough to take his superior mode of transportation. "We have to move."

Dad's head bobs loosely on his neck as he hurries in front of Jesse. He points toward the front of the hospital. "I'm parked in the physician's lot. They won't look for you there, and we can take the exit out onto Fourth Street and get on the highway going north." He breaks into a run that seems absurdly slow after how fast Jesse and I have been moving the past few hours.

It takes forever to reach the staff parking lot, but we finally make it to Dad's beige Mercedes without any shots being fired. The main entrance to the hospital is just visible from the lot. I stand on tiptoe to get a better look, but I don't see either of the fake FBI agents standing outside.

Where have they gone? They've had plenty of time to get to the ground floor. Did the hospital security hear the gunshots and go investigate? Did they call the police? Even if the Coffee Nurse is in on this, surely the entire hospital isn't cool with people shooting guns in a place of healing.

Coffee Nurse. My dad knows her. Or *did* know her, anyway, back when I was in the hospital. How did she get involved with terrorists? And what do terrorists have to do with me and Jesse? I make a mental note to grill Dad on everything as soon as we get on the road. I need answers before I'll go to any "safe house" with him. So far he's done a pretty lousy job of keeping anyone safe.

Which reminds me…

"Where's Penny, Dad?" I ask as I circle around the car. It would be just like Dad to forget my stepmother could be in danger, too. "Did you call—"

"Penny's already on her way to the safe house," Dad says. "She's calling some of her old FBI friends to see if we can find out more about the people involved in this. Apparently someone hired Vince to steal some of my old research."

"We know," I say. "We saw him at the house this morning. He tried to kidnap me and Jesse at the bus station."

"But Dani broke his nose and we got away." The pride in Jesse's voice makes me stand up straighter as he opens the passenger's door for me and runs around to the driver's side.

I guess Dad is stuck with the back seat—another thing he'd usually never tolerate. But when I glance over my shoulder, he's sliding in and buckling his seat belt. I meet his eyes and he smiles that rare smile he reserves for me and Penny, the one that softens him into someone who looks like part of a family, a man who knows how to love.

That smile has never seemed so much like a lie.

"I'm glad you fought back. I'm so glad I found you, Dani," he says as Jesse starts the car and backs out. "I was scared to death that you...that something had happened."

I turn back around to face the front, not trusting myself to speak. I'm too angry and confused and sad. How could he have done this? How could he have lied to me for years, how could he have let me think...

"Did you know the truth when I was little?" I keep my eyes on the road as Jesse pulls onto Fourth Street and steers the car toward the freeway. "Did you know that I wasn't crazy? That Rachel was real?"

"Rachel isn't real." His voice takes on that condescending, I-am-a-brilliant-scientist-and-you-can-barely-pass-Algebra tone that I know all too well. I grit my teeth until my jaw aches. "The things the Dream Project kids believe they see are psychic projections, a form of subconscious telekinesis accredited to the—"

"The Dream Project," Jesse interrupts. "That sounds like more people than just me and Dani."

"Yes, there are...others." Dad has the decency to sound a little ashamed of himself. But only a little. "We needed a diverse group to accurately evaluate the results of the medication, but I promise you we never imagined this was going to happen. We thought the treatment was going to be the best thing that happened to any of you. The best thing that ever happened to the human race. That's why we called it the Dream Project. We had a dream that the children we treated would never suffer from sickness or disease again. We wanted you to be the healthiest, happiest, strongest generation the world has ever known. A superior race of people."

I shiver. In eighth grade history, we did an entire unit on the holocaust; Hitler wanted a superior race of people, too, and he hadn't been above experimenting on children to find out what separated the strong from the weak. The monstrous acts of torture performed by Nazi "scientists" make Dad and the other doctors who tested their medicine on us seem like okay people. But the fact that I have to compare my father to some of the most evil men in history in order to make his behavior less horrifying isn't comforting.

"We thought we were giving you all a priceless gift," Dad concludes.

Jesse snorts. "So what went wrong?"

"Nothing went wrong. At first," Dad says. "For a few months we thought it was going to be a success. The sick kids were getting well and the well kids were getting bigger, stronger, healing more quickly." He sighs, a tortured sound that I suspect has more to do with his failed wonder drug than any real remorse. "But then we started seeing elevated white blood cell counts in the daily blood work.

The meds were causing the patients' immune systems to become overactive. We were worried, but over the course of a few weeks the problem seemed to resolve itself. We started thinking we might have found a cure for autoimmune disease, arthritis, cancer…Then the psychotic episodes started. In every patient. Across the board. They were especially violent in those who were healthy at the start of the trial."

Like Jesse. Is that the reason his dragon went in for the kill right away? Is that the reason his imaginary enemy is still so much bigger and stronger than mine?

"But we weren't psychotic," Jesse whispers.

His eyes are fixed on the road and his fingers grip the steering wheel so tight the veins stand out on the back of his hands. This has to be even harder for him to hear. At least I was sick to start with, and my father was the one who decided I should join the Dream Project. But Jesse was just…stolen.

I want to reach out to him, but I'm suddenly very conscious of my dad watching my every move from the back seat. I don't want him to know about Jesse and me. He doesn't deserve to know anything about my life. Not anymore.

"No," Dad says. "It was a manifestation of an autoimmune disorder that we'd never seen before."

"An autoimmune disorder caused by the medicine," I say, needing Dad to take responsibility instead of blaming some disorder like he had nothing to do with it.

"Not exactly," he says. "The Dream treatment actually altered the patients' genetic material, creating an auto-immune disorder that caused their minds to manufacture imaginary…assassins."

Jesse glowers at Dad in the rearview mirror. "That sounds like crazy to me. You're still saying these things are all in our heads."

"Well…" Dad sniffs. "These beings *don't* exist out-side your imagination, but their actions do manifest in the real world. We've got hours of video of objects floating through the air with nothing there to hold them, wet ani-mal footprints coming out of hospital bathrooms, elevated temperatures in rooms where the kids imagined—"

"So you *did* know that I wasn't crazy," I say, trying not to think too hard about what he's just said. He's all but admitted that he let people tape kids being attacked and didn't even try to help, but I can't think about that right now. I can't imagine my father watching Rachel come for me with a hypodermic needle and leaving me to fight it out on my own without wanting to kick him out of the car. While it's moving. "You knew that Rachel was your fault."

"Dani, I was the first to say that I thought what was happening to you was a result of the medication. Don't you remember that I—"

"I remember that you and Mom made me talk to that psychiatrist for months, even though you knew it wouldn't help." Another horrible thought rises in my mind. "Did Mom know? Did she know you were using me as—"

"I wasn't using you," Dad says, loud enough to make

me press myself against the car door. "I was trying to save your life!"

"Did Mom know?" I demand again.

"Your mom didn't know anything," his says, voice softer, but just as bitter as it always is when we talk about Mom. "She didn't care what happened as long as she didn't have to make any grown-up decisions."

His words sting more than they should. I know my mom isn't a responsible grown-up. That's the reason she lives in Philadelphia with a boyfriend half her age and hasn't had a job in sixteen years. That's why I've never spent more than a couple of weeks at a time at her place every summer instead of the six weeks mandated in my parents' divorce decree. She can't handle the responsibility. But she loves me. I can't believe she would have been okay with Dad doing what he did—to me or the other kids in his "project."

"And no, I *didn't* know that psychiatric therapy wouldn't help." Dad leans between the seats, getting as close to looking me in the face as he can while I'm refusing to turn around. "We were dealing with an entirely new phenomenon, and the human brain is a mystery at the best of times. I hoped Dr. Messing would be able to help you gain control of your mind, and of Rachel."

I hesitate, the angry words on my lips slipping back into my throat. I *have* started to gain control of Rachel, but only today, years and years after her initial appearance and with no help from a psychiatrist.

"So, why are they back?" I ask. "Why are they attacking Jesse and me again? Why are they so much stronger?"

"And why did someone run our bus off the road?" Jesse asks. "Why are terrorists trying to kill us?"

"I don't think they're trying to kill you." Dad's voice is thinner, weaker than it was when he was talking about the experiment. "I can't be sure, but I imagine they considered the accident a calculated risk. It could have killed you, or it could have been the kind of traumatic event needed to reactivate your unique autoimmune disease."

Reactivate? It sounds like we're robots or something. "What about the medication? Wouldn't we have to be taking the same drugs again?"

"Not necessarily," Dad says. "When we finally managed to get all the kids into remission, there was some concern that the disease could be reactivated by events that trigger other autoimmune diseases—a serious infection, a broken bone, things of that nature. But after a few years it didn't seem like that was happening. The only time any former patient had a relapse was after a car accident. The little girl suffered significant head trauma, and afterward, she…"

He leans his head against his hand, and when he speaks again there is genuine sorrow in his voice. "She checked into another hospital after the crash and was killed in her bed two days later. She was strangled in her sleep by something the security monitors couldn't see. The hospital staff assumed there must have been a camera malfunction and the police opened an investigation, but they never found her killer."

I don't say anything. I don't know what to say. Maybe it wasn't his intention, but Dad just confirmed that some of the kids like us have lost their battle. We could lose, too. *Jesse* could lose.

"I think the people who are after you came into possession of that information," Dad says, "And they decided if it worked once, it might work again."

"Okay, so maybe that's why they wrecked the bus," Jesse says. "But what about the guns? I've got a bullet in my shoulder. That has nothing to do with head trauma."

Dad sighs again. "I don't know. Maybe they've guessed that you've been reactivated and you're stronger and faster and capable of healing just about any damage done to your body. In our original trials, the teenagers we treated displayed amazing athletic and healing powers. These men could think that a gunshot wound is the only way to slow you down long enough to catch you."

"And maybe they don't care if they take us alive," I say. Agent Bullock had been trying to kill us. I'd seen the look in his eyes.

"I think they want you alive," Dad says. "At least some of you. They obviously want to see if reactivating the treatment in older adolescents is successful. They can't do that if you're all dead."

The matter-of-fact way he discusses my life or death makes me shiver. Who is this man? And how did I ever believe he loved me, even in his own peculiar way?

"Initially, the teenagers in the original trials were our brightest hope," Dad continues, his voice tired. "They were so strong and had a superhuman ability to heal. But most of them had to be taken off their meds in the first few weeks. There were…deadly elevations in body temperature. They started rejecting the gene modification and we couldn't bring the fevers down in time."

"So are you saying…" I stare dumbly out the window, watching the city turn into countryside while my pulse thuds ominously in my temple. I can't even finish the sentence. Have Jesse and I made it through everything we've been through today only to learn we're going to die of a fever?

"I don't know." Dad puts a hand on my shoulder. I cringe closer to the door. He pulls away and doesn't try to touch me again. "But I'm going to do everything I can do to make sure you're okay. And there's a chance that reactivating the altered DNA of teenagers or adults who received the treatment as children might not cause the same side effects. We'll have to monitor you both closely over the next few weeks."

"I'm not a scientist. Obviously." Jesse's voice is strung tight. He steps on the gas, pulling in front of a station wagon full of happy-looking kids. "But I paid enough attention in Bio last year to know that gene modification and altered DNA aren't things that happen when you're trying to treat an illness. Let alone super powers and super healing and all the other stuff. What kind of *medicine* were you giving us?"

Dad clears his throat. "We weren't trying to treat an illness, we were trying to eliminate the possibility of illness. We were trying to make you…invulnerable."

I pull my knees to my chest, hugging them tight. My mind races faster than the wheels speeding down the interstate beneath us. Invulnerable. Strong. Altered DNA. Experiments. Psychic Phenomenon. Terrorists. The pieces of the puzzle swirl around and around until they begin to form a chilling picture. I can only think of one reason terrorists would want genetically altered, super-strong, hard-to-damage teenagers capable of doing impossible things with their minds.

"They want to use us as some kind of weapon. Right?" I ask, letting my gaze slide over to watch Jesse's reaction. His eyes meet mine just long enough for me to see that he's already worked through the logic and come to the same conclusion.

"I wouldn't imagine they want to use you or Jesse specifically. But if teenagers modified when they were children and reactivated after puberty can deal with the side effects of the Dream treatment, and still retain the same positive traits as the first test subjects…" Dad trails off as he falls back into his seat. "But you said you've already been attacked by your psychic manifestations. Are these the same ones from when you were children? Have you seen them once or—"

"A few times. But we're starting to get control over them. Like you said." I silently pray that I'm telling the truth, and that Jesse will be able to handle his dragon when it shows up again.

"If that's the case, then…"

"Then the people who are after us will want to grow their own crop," Jesse says, speaking the words my dad is unwilling to utter. "That's why they want all your research, right? So they can make their own superhuman terrorists in a few years?"

"I'm sure they'll find a lot of people willing to sign their children up for the treatment," Dad says. "Especially parents who know their children will die without it. That's why I did this, Danielle. I wanted you to have a chance to grow up. Even if that meant you'd grow up to hate me."

I look out the window and pretend I didn't hear him. Do I hate him? I don't know. A part of me can understand why he made the choice he did for me, but I can't forgive him for Jesse. Jesse didn't have a choice, and he would have had a better chance at a happy life if they'd left him alone.

They. Who are *they*? How many adults are in on this?

"Does everyone at North Corp know about the experiments?" I ask. "Or is it just you and your research team? And what about the people at the hospital? At least some of the doctors and nurses must have—"

"I can't discuss any of that, Dani. The identities of the people involved in the project are classified."

"Like, national-security classified?" Jesse asks. "Is this some kind of government thing?"

Dad's steady stream of word-vomit ceases for the first

time since we got in the car. I finally turn to look at him again, but his eyes are on the hands clenched in his lap.

"Is that how you met Penny?" I ask. Dad told me that he and Penny met at a North Corp banquet. Penny's dad was a big North Corp supporter before he died a few years ago. They even have a building named after him. "Is she part of this?"

"Penny…" Dad sniffs, but it isn't until he lifts his face that I realize he's crying. "I think Penny's going to leave me." I'm too shocked by the tears streaming down Dad's cheeks to know what to say. I've never seen him cry, not even when he thought I was going to die.

"She didn't know about any of this, but I had to tell her today. To keep her safe." Dad swipes the back of his hand across his face. "She was so angry and disappointed. I think she's going to ask for a divorce."

"I'm sorry." And I am. I *am* sorry. I don't want to lose Penny. She's a part of my family who I've taken for granted for way too long. "Maybe she'll…maybe she'll be able to forgive you."

Dad is silent for a moment. "Maybe. But you never will. Will you?"

I look at Jesse again, at this boy who was used and thrown away, and shake my head. No, I don't think I'll ever be able to forgive my dad. Not ever. Not even if I really believed he was sorry.

Fifteen

Jesse

I know I should be angry. My insides should be on fire. I've pounded faces for offenses way more minor than what this man has done. I should pull over and beat him senseless.

But I don't. I just keep driving, following his directions off the interstate and up a two-lane road that gets narrower as it winds through giant pine forests covered in snow. We need Dr. Connor. I have a hell of a lot more questions, we don't know how to get to the safe house without him, and no matter how evil and full of it he is, he's still Dani's dad.

No matter how many lives he's wrecked, no matter how many kids he's damaged, no matter what kind of freaky, experimental shit he's a part of—that's never going to go away. He's her father, and I won't give him any more power. If I hurt him, Dani will always remember it.

She thinks she hates her dad right now, but she'll hate me more if I hurt him. I don't want her to hate me. I want her to keep looking at me with that crazy intense look that makes my entire body hum, that makes me want to stay right next to her…forever. I've never felt like this before. About anyone. Not even my sister, who's the only other person I can remember loving in a normal, uncomplicated kind of way.

But I don't love Dani like a sister. I love her like an answer I never thought I'd find, a solution I didn't believe existed.

I'm so crazy about her a part of me is actually glad we're on our way to some super-secret FBI compound. I hate cops and I'm pretty sure I'll hate federal cops just as much, but at least I'll be close to her all the time. We'll never have to go home to our separate houses or head down different paths to the boys' and girls' campuses at school.

I have a feeling we won't be going back to school or our old lives at all. I know I should be scared about that, too—I could lose my chance at an athletic scholarship and the bright future I've worked so hard for—but I'm not. The only thing that scares me is that I might lose Dani, that I might hurt her.

But maybe I can learn to control the dragon. What Dani made Rachel do in the hospital proves it's possible. I just need to figure out how she's doing it…

I glance in the rearview mirror. We've been on the road for three hours, and the late afternoon light has made the whole world sleepy and still. Dani's dad hasn't said a word since she shut him down on the whole "forgiveness" thing, and his eyes are closed. But no matter how nap-inducing this ride has been, I'm not going to count on him being asleep. It's better if Dani and I keep our voices down. I don't want him to find out how dangerous I am. I'm amazed he let me drive, but I guess he assumes our imaginary "friends" are still playing by the old rules and only show up when we're alone.

"So how do you do it?" I whisper. "How do you get Rachel to do what you say?"

"I don't know…I just…" Dani glances over her shoulder, taking in her dad's apparently sleeping form before turning back to me. "I decided I was in control and told her she needed to listen. I kept thinking about how I talk to kids when I'm babysitting and they start doing stuff I know they're not supposed to. I know that sounds stupid, but—"

"No, it doesn't." I know the power of a good bluff. It's just never crossed my mind to try that with the Thing. I've never considered using reason with a creature that spends most of its time hissing and snapping. "So Rachel understands you when you talk?"

"Yeah. And she talks to me sometimes. I can hear her voice in my head."

"The Thing isn't big on using its words."

"Right." Dani's lips curve up. She takes a thoughtful bite of the Power Bar she fished out of her dad's glove compartment a few minutes ago. I clench my stomach muscles, trying to keep my gut from rumbling as she chews.

She offered me half the bar, but I said I wasn't hungry. The last time I ate, the dragon made an appearance not long after. I don't want to take the chance that feeding myself feeds the Thing until I have some clue how to keep it from hurting anyone.

"So it might not listen to words. I don't know. And it might be harder for you, anyway," Dani says. "Remember what Dad said about the psychic manifestations being worse for the kids who weren't sick? Maybe that's happening now. Like…the energy it takes for my body to correct the diabetes leaves less energy for Rachel? Or something?"

"But she's stronger today, right? Stronger than she was when you were little?"

Dani nods, and takes another quick look over her shoulder before leaning over to whisper in my ear. "She showed up in the back seat a few minutes ago, but I made her go away without saying anything. The Thing hasn't shown up, has it?"

I shake my head. "That's why I'm not eating. Starve the body, starve the monster."

"And maybe your shoulder has something to do with it. The energy it takes to heal you could be draining the Thing's strength." Her fingers trail across my back, making me shiver. "How does it feel?"

"Better, but not totally better." I roll my shoulder, wincing as a ghost of the original pain stabs through the bone. "I think I'll need a doctor to dig the bullet out sooner or later."

"You're also going to have to eat something sooner or later."

The conversation dies a quick death—the realization that the Thing will be back and I'll have to deal with it hanging in the air between us. Finally, Dani leans close enough that I can feel her lips brush my ear when she whispers, "I'm not going to let them know that I can make Rachel do things. Only that I can make her go away. The more I think about it, the more I think that the terrorists might not be the only ones who'd like to use what we can do."

I nod. I've been thinking the same thing. But the fact remains that I *can't* make the Thing do what I say. I can't control it at all yet. Sooner or later the people in charge at this safe house are going to realize this, and I can imagine what will happen then. I'll wind up in a cage, locked away, just like Vince said I would. Good guys or bad guys, the ending will be the same.

"You can do this," Dani says, as if she can read my mind. "You *have* to do this."

"I know." My voice is so soft I can barely hear it. "Or people are going to die."

Dani's voice is even softer. "I'll die if anything happens to you." It makes my chest ache. Her words should have sounded silly, melodramatic. But they don't. Not to me. Because I know exactly how she feels. We're like those crazy people who fall in love in rehab because they've finally found someone as messed up as they are. Dani is the only person who has ever made me feel like I'm not alone. I would love her for that even if she weren't beautiful and good and brave.

"Don't leave me, okay?" Her hand curls at the back of my neck. "No matter what."

"I won't. I promise."

She presses a kiss to my cheek before sliding back into her seat. I fight to keep my hands on the wheel. We haven't said the words, but we might as well have. She loves me. I love her. It's insane and impossible and...right. I want to pull the car over and kiss her until she's breathless, to hold her so tight we can't tell where one of us stops and the other starts, to run my hands over every inch of her until I know beyond a doubt that she's real and mine and—

"We're going to need to turn soon," Dani's dad pipes up from the back seat, a hard note in his voice, as if he knows I was all over his daughter in my mind a second ago. "Look for a sign for the Evergreen Retreats. We'll be meeting our pickup team at cabin number thirteen."

"Lucky number thirteen." My lame attempt at a joke makes Dani "mmph," but her dad stays silent. When I look at him in the rearview mirror, he's staring out the window, his face pinched tight.

He looks so...scared. Sad. Worried. Not like a man who has nearly made it to safety. But then, he just had to tell his wife and daughter that he's a mad scientist and both of them hate his guts. It probably isn't his best day ever. He hasn't been chased by invisible killing machines, but he's lost a lot and had some face time with the bad guys with guns.

Bad guys. *With guns.* Just how *did* he escape the bad guys with guns?

The gnawing in my stomach turns to a cold lump of fear. My foot eases off the gas, slow and steady, not enough to attract attention but enough to slow our progress toward the Evergreen Retreats.

"So, you said someone ran you off the road?" I ask, raising my voice so Dr. Connor will know I'm talking to him. "The car's driving good. Where did they hit you?"

"They didn't hit me," he says without hesitation. Still, something in his voice makes the hairs at the back of my neck prickle. I feel a lie slipping over the seats, wrapping around my throat. "I pulled over when they fired at my tires. They drove past and got stuck on the bridge."

"Didn't they come back for you?" I ask, trying to sound casual.

He leans between the seats and squints at the road. "I'm assuming so, but I lost them in the city."

I nod and ease off the gas a little more, pretending to look for the sign. "And you didn't run into them again?"

"No. I didn't." Dr. Connor is finally starting to sound frustrated with my questions, but that's just fine. He can stay frustrated. And we'll stay away from our pickup point until my bullshit meter stops screaming.

I slam on the brake and pull to the side of the road, coming to a sharp stop. Dani's seat belt catches and holds, and Dr. Connor grunts and braces himself to keep from falling into the front seat.

"What's wrong?" he asks, not bothering to hide his anger. "You could have hurt someone." He reaches a hand out to touch Dani's shoulder. I fight the urge to slap it away. He doesn't deserve to touch her, not if my suspicions are correct. "Are you okay, sweetheart?"

"I'm fine," Dani says, lifting curious eyes to mine.

"So how did you find out your cell phone had a tracking device inside?" I shift the car into park and turn in my seat, meeting Dr. Connor's stare straight on.

"What?"

"If the guys with guns never found you again, how did you find out there was a tracking device in your phone?"

He pauses for less than a second, but that's all it takes for his guilt to be confirmed. At least in my mind. I have no doubt that whatever he says from here on out is going to be a lie.

"How else would they have found me?" he asks.

I shrug, and casually reach for the button to my seat belt. I have a feeling I'm going to want to be free to move. Very soon. "I don't know." The button clicks and my belt snakes across my chest. "Maybe they'd been watching you for a while? Don't you always go to work at the same time every day? And take the same road?"

"Maybe." Dr. Connor's fingers dig into the back of Dani's seat. He glances in the rearview and stares a little too long, like he's hoping for another car to show up and encourage me to pull back on the road. But we haven't seen another car in almost an hour.

"I mean…I'm not super-smart or anything…" I look over at Dani. She's sitting absolutely still, watching her dad like snakes are about to start crawling out of his mouth. She knows. She's guessed what I've guessed.

I turn back to Dr. Connor. "But, a tracking device wouldn't have been my first guess. Anyone who watches me long enough is going to know that I walk up Bean Street at about seven twenty-five every Monday through Friday. Right?"

"I have no idea." He looks at the rearview again. "I'm unaware of your daily routine."

"Really? So you didn't help those guys figure out when our bus would be leaving for the city? Or where they needed to be with that semi to hit us at the right moment?"

"You're out of your mind," he says. "I would never—"

"So you're just in charge of helping pick up the pieces, then?" A flicker of recognition sparks behind Dr. Connor's square glasses and every muscle in my body tenses.

He looks afraid, but not of me. He's afraid of something else, something—

"I would do anything to protect my daughter," he says.

Dani sucks in a breath.

That son of a bitch. That lousy son of a bitch. No wonder those men at the hospital disappeared. They must have known that Dani's dad was on the job and we'd be delivered right into their hands by the end of the day. Way back in the woods, where no one will care how many times they fire their weapons or how loud we scream.

"Dad, no." Dani cringes as far away from her dad as her seat belt will allow. "What have you done? What—"

"Listen. You have to listen." Dr. Connor ignores Dani, his eyes all on me. "You seem to have feelings for my daughter. If you really care about her, then you have—"

"You don't know what I feel! You—Shit!" I slam my fists into the back of my seat. The car suddenly feels too small. I need room to move, to rage, to work out the betrayal squirming inside of me before I smash this bastard's face in.

I grab the door and open it only to slam it shut again with a growl. There isn't time to get out and punch at a bunch of trees. We have to get out of here. We have to get off this isolated road and headed for someplace the people after us won't think to look. But where?

I rack my brain, trying to think of the best way out. It's hours back to the main highway and what if we run into Agent Bullock or the Man in Gray on the way? They have to know this is where we're headed. But I have no idea how far this road goes on from here, or if there's a border crossing station when it finally runs into Canada, or if we'll be able to get *across* the border without passports if there—

"Please," Dani's dad says. "Please. Just keep driving."

I laugh, a nasty sound I don't bother trying to keep inside. "You're insane." I reach for the gearshift, but freeze when something cold and hard presses against the base of my skull.

"Keep driving north, Jesse. Make the turn into the Evergreen Retreats and find cabin thirteen." Dr. Connor keeps the gun tight against my head. "Or I will shoot you.

These people already have some of the others. They don't care if you come to them dead or alive. I'd rather not kill you, but in the end...that's your choice."

My choice. As if this man has ever given me a choice.

Sixteen

Dani

My dad is a bad guy. My dad is a bad guy. My dad is a bad guy. The litany thrums dumbly through my head as Jesse shifts the car into drive. I can't make sense of it, can't believe that my bicycle-riding, organic-food-eating, "I refuse to use a cell phone because technology is bad for the brain" dad has really pulled a gun from his coat pocket and plans to deliver Jesse and me to the people who've been hunting us.

It's only after Jesse eases the car back onto the road—moving us closer to the other bad guys waiting at the end of the ride—that I remember how to speak.

"Dad, please. Put the gun down," I say. "You can't do this."

"I'm sorry, Dani." He sounds like he really *is* sorry, even as his finger whitens on the trigger. I can see the indecision twitching around his jaw. He's thinking about putting a bullet in Jesse's brain, whether that might be easier than letting him live.

Dad likes things easy. It's why he dumped Mom and married a relentlessly upbeat, old-fashioned woman like Penny who devotes herself to him when he's home but doesn't care if he's really married to his job. It's why I've done my best to fly under his radar, to be the good girl who gets good grades and doesn't make trouble. I didn't want to live with Mom, and a part of me knew that Dad would only keep me with him if I was easy.

Jesse isn't easy. At all.

The sour taste of fear rushes into my throat. "Don't do it, Dad. Don't shoot him! I'll kill you if you do, I swear to God I will."

"No, Dani. You're not going to hurt anyone," he says, turning to me with tears shining in his eyes. "I'm not going to let them turn you into something you're not. There's no way to reverse the changes in your DNA, but we'll find a way to put you back into remission. We'll get your head on straight and—"

"My head *is* on straight." Anger burns brighter than my fear. My hands ball into fists I'm not sure I know what to do with. With Vince, sure, but with my dad... Can I really hit him? Can I risk the chance that lashing out at him might make his finger squeeze a little tighter? "Dad. This is murder. Think about it."

"We'll start a new life somewhere, just you and me, far away from everything," he says, ignoring me the way he always has. "Maybe South America. Or Alaska. You said you wanted to go to Alaska and see the whales, when you were little. Do you remember that?"

"I'm not going to Alaska. I'm not going anywhere with you. I won't let you do this to Jesse!"

"I don't have a choice." The hopeful note in Dad's voice withers and dies. "They were going to take you both. The only way I could keep you safe is to give them all my research on the Dream Project and a test subject." His gun twitches to the right and then back again. "Turn up there. Just after the sign."

"Jesse is not a *test subject*. He's a person. Please, listen to yourself. You—"

"Danielle, don't—"

"And I love him, Dad." The car slows. Jesse looks at me. The barrel of Dad's gun now presses right up against his cheek. "I love him," I repeat, staring into those bright, clear eyes that let me right into the heart of him. I know that he feels the same way. He loves me too, no matter how crazy it seems to fall so hard for someone you barely know.

But I feel like I've known Jesse forever, like I've been waiting for him my entire life. He's what was missing when I lay awake in the dark, wondering if I was crazy, praying that someone would see the monster that came in the night. He's the only person who knows what that feels like, the only person who has ever believed in my weakness and my strength and made me believe that I'm tough enough to fight back. With Jesse, I know that I can banish the nightmares and become something more than a damaged person ruled by fear.

Without him…

I can't imagine life without him. I *won't* imagine it.

"Stop this, Dad. This is the last time I'm going to ask."

It's all I can do not to reach for the gun and pull it from his hand. But what if he shoots Jesse before I can get it? The thought of losing Jesse, of those blue eyes closing forever, is more terrifying than anything. More terrifying than dying of diabetes, more terrifying than Rachel and her mouth full of blood.

Rachel.

"Keep driving." Dad's sole focus is the gun trained on Jesse's neck. "Turn here."

My throat gets tighter and tighter as Jesse pulls down the dirt road. Evergreens grow thick on both sides, pressing in on the car, smothering the last of my options. This is it. Dad has given me no choice. I can't let him do this, I can't let him bring us a second closer to cabin thirteen and the people waiting to take Jesse away.

Rachel. Rachel! I scream her name in my mind, willing her to show herself. I imagine her shining hair, her mean little eyes. She came to me when I needed her in the hospital.

Still, I'm shocked when she winks into sight above my dad's shoulder. I'm even more shocked by how *happy* I am to see her. After so many years of dreading her appearance, it feels wrong to be grateful to see that gaping red mouth, those cunning hands that reach out to flick Dad's collar.

Dad jumps and turns to look over his shoulder. His

finger tightens on the trigger, making my heart surge into my throat. *If you make him hurt Jesse, you will never come out to play again.*

Rachel sticks out her tongue. *Who says I like to play, stupid? I'm not a baby anymore.*

You love to play, and I know the games you like best.

I meet Dad's eyes, trying to remember his face, some part of me certain this will be the last time I'll ever see it. No matter how many horrible things I've found out about him in the past few hours, tears still sting the backs of my eyes and my voice trembles as I say, "Good-bye."

Really? Daddy dearest? Rachel's giggle ties her words up with a bow.

"Danielle, don't even think about getting out of this car," Dad warns. "Stay right there." I don't answer, just blink, sending tears running down my cheeks.

Get the gun and get him out of the car. Hurt him as much as you have to, I tell Rachel. *But don't kill him…unless there's no other choice.*

Ah, not fair. You never let me kill anything! Rachel wrinkles her nose, but I can see the excitement dancing in her eyes.

Seconds later, she has Dad's wrist in her fists. She jerks his hand toward the ceiling before wrenching it in a sharp circle. I hear the snap of cracking bone and the gun falls to the seat as Dad starts to scream, a raw, tortured sound that rips at things inside of me. He's in horrible pain. It's clear in every tight line of his body, in his clawed hands, pale face, wide wailing mouth.

And it's my fault. *I* am doing this. *I* broke my dad's wrist and now I'm slamming his head into the car door, again and again, wringing more pitiful cries from his throat every time his skull collides with the leather-covered metal.

I'm not consciously telling Rachel what to do—which bones to break, how many times to bash Dad's head before throwing open the car door—but I'm in control. If what Dad told us is true, my mind—or my messed-up immune system, or *something* inside of me—made Rachel. She's a part of me, a deadly, awful part that laughs as she hurls my father out onto the ground, sending blood spraying across the white snow.

"Call her off, Dani." Jesse lunges over the seat, grabbing the door Rachel opened and slamming it closed. "You'll hate yourself if you kill him."

"I told her not to kill him," I whisper, wiping at the tears rushing down my face. "I just…I don't think I can stop her." I watch Rachel grab fistfuls of Dad's hair and lift him like he weighs less than the dolls we once played with together. She hurls him deeper into the forest. He hits a tree trunk and slides into the snow, but there isn't time for him to regain his feet before Rachel has skipped over to greet his face with her fist. I can feel how full she still is—full of hate and anger and the need to punish this man for playing God. "She's not finished."

Jesse cups my cheek and gently turns my face toward him. "She's finished when you say she's finished." His eyes meet mine, penetrating the fog. "You're the boss, right?"

I nod. His touch makes me stronger, the way it has since the second I sat down next to him on the bus this morning, back when I was a semi-normal girl feeling anxious about being abandoned by my best friend.

Now my best friend is dead along with half my school, and my dad threatened to kill the boy I love right in front of me. Anger—white hot and pure in its intensity—flares inside me again. It isn't Rachel who isn't finished. *I'm* not finished. A part of me wants Rachel to keep hitting Dad until he hurts more, until he pays a bigger price, maybe the ultimate price. But the rest of me knows Jesse is right.

I want to get away from the scary people. I don't want to become one.

I turn back to Rachel, focusing on her flying fists, willing her to stop. After one last blow—a punch to the face that sends Dad arcing through the air to land on his back—she does. She wipes her hands on her clothes, smearing bloody fingerprints over her softly rounded belly like a kid who's just finished a messy piece of pizza.

But that red turning black against the fabric of her dress isn't pizza sauce.

Way yummier than pizza sauce. Rachel lifts a finger to her mouth and licks.

For a moment, I swear I can taste the metallic flavor of my father's blood on my tongue. I gag, dry heaving as my hands fly to cover my mouth. *Go away! You're done. Go away!*

Now who's the baby? she asks. But when I open my eyes, she's gone, vanished into the cold air. A few feet away from where she stood, my dad pushes up onto his hands and knees and lifts his swollen face to watch Jesse drive away.

"She's gone." I sit back and buckle my seat belt, but I can't keep myself from finding Dad's reflection in the rearview mirror. He looks so small, so entirely beaten. I bite my lip. I refuse to feel sorry for him or to think about what might happen to him out here in the woods, with the early winter night approaching and the temperature dropping close to zero.

"He'll be okay. The cabins can't be far," Jesse says. "He'll get inside one of them and be able to call for help. Or at least make a fire and stay warm."

"Right." I thread my fingers together and hold on tight, trying to keep my hands from shaking. It feels like a thousand butterflies have been freed beneath my skin. Their wings beat frantically against my heart and lungs as they try to find a way out, but they can't. They're trapped. Just like me.

Now that the anger is gone, there's only fear, desperation. It feels like I'm falling and falling and I don't know when I'm going to stop. I've lost my dad, and my best friend, and my life as I knew it. Jesse and I can't ever go home again. Not ever.

I wonder if he knows.

"We should head north and try to get across the border," Jesse says as he pulls out onto the main road. "If we have to, we can cross on foot and walk until we find a town. We should get some new clothes and dye our hair or something. Try to make it harder for them to find us while we figure out what to do next."

He knows.

"We can move a lot faster than they can, so we won't freeze on the way through the woods. And maybe crossing the border will buy us some time." He pushes the car faster, faster, until our speed starts to feel dangerous.

My stomach flips over and my brain demands that I tell Jesse to slow down, but I don't. We'll be fine. Even if we crash. My brain is still living in the old Danielle, the one who didn't have supernatural powers, who couldn't run like a gazelle or heal a gunshot wound in less than an hour or beat people bloody with her new imaginary weapon.

Not people. *Dad.* Dad is back there. Beaten. Hurting. *Because of me.*

My throat closes up and more tears sting into my eyes as I turn to look back. I know I won't see him, but still... I have to look back. One last time.

It's a good thing I do. I'm sure Jesse would have noticed it eventually, but maybe not as soon as I have. Soon enough to give us a chance.

"Someone's back there," I say. "A car."

It's the only other car we've seen for several hours, a sleek black machine with shining bug-eye headlights that glow orange in the gray light. It doesn't look like a car that belongs to someone heading north for a weekend in the wilderness during the coldest part of the year. It looks like a car made for going fast, going unnoticed, getting in and out without anyone remembering it at the scene of the crime.

Jesse grunts and pushes the pedal even closer to the floor. Behind us, the black car speeds faster, keeping up, even gaining a few feet.

"Shit," Jesse says, obviously coming to the same conclusion. There's only one reason the car behind us is on this road. The hunt for Jesse and Dani isn't over.

"It's the men from the hospital." The outline of the two men in the car swims into focus. "I can't see their faces, but it has to be them."

"We can't be that far from the border." Jesse gives the car more gas and the engine groans. "Maybe there will be someone there."

"Someone who will think those guys are FBI agents and we're stupid kids who've done something illegal." I cling to the handle over the window as Jesse whips around the next curve. The wheels barely stay on the road. "Even if they believe us, Agent Bullock already shot that nurse at the hospital. I don't think he cares if—"

"So you think we should take care of this before we get to the border?"

My mouth opens and closes. Is that what I think? I don't know. All I know is that I'm scared, and only getting more scared as Jesse reaches for the gun Dad dropped into the front seat.

"You think you can bring Rachel back?" he asks.

Can I? Does he want me to kill someone with Rachel? Is he going to kill someone with that gun? Do we have any other choice?

"Dani?"

I nod. "I can. I'm ready." I'm not, but that doesn't matter. If today has taught me anything, it's that life—and death—don't wait for you to be ready.

Seventeen

Jesse

I force down the acid rising in my throat, ignore the pulse pounding in my ears and the terror creeping across my skin.

I saw it a few minutes back—a flash of green in the shadows under the trees, a spot of red in the frozen snow. The Thing. Starving myself isn't going to hold it off much longer. It's coming. It could be here any second. I can feel it, like a muscle ready to rip and take me out of the game.

Maybe it'll jump onto the car and burst through the windshield like last time. Or maybe it'll pop up in the back seat, lean over, and rip out Dani's throat before I can pull my hands from the wheel. I can almost see the way her blood will splash onto the dash as the dragon comes for me and the car spins out of control.

No. You're in control. You won't let it hurt her. You won't let anything hurt her.

"Get ready. I'm going to turn the car to face them as

soon as I get the chance." I grip the wheel tight as we zip around another sharp curve. "But don't get out of the car unless you have to. It'll give us some cover if they start shooting."

"Okay," she says, her voice not much more than a whisper.

I risk a quick look over at her side of the car. Dani is as white as the snow flashing past outside. What she did to her dad really messed her up. I have to get her somewhere safe where we can eat and rest and I can convince her that we're going to be all right. Maybe a hotel, something small on the Canadian side of the border.

The thought of spending the night with Dani, of holding her until her breath slows and she falls asleep in my arms, is enough to send a rush of determination surging inside me. I want that night with her. I want every night and all the days in between. I want to be the one to keep her safe, to be the person she can count on no matter what happens.

But before I can promise her safety, I have to prove myself. Sooner or later, I'll have to face the Thing and show it who's boss. I just hope I won't have to show it right now, while Dani and I are being chased by a couple of flesh-and-blood killers. With guns.

God. Do I even know how to use this kind of gun? I think I do, at least well enough to keep the bullets flying in the right direction. It's a handgun, semi-automatic, and more proof that Dani's dad is a lot more dangerous than he looks. I could tell he was thinking about blowing my brains out for a while there. Maybe he would have, if Dani hadn't brought Rachel in to kick his ass.

Too bad that doesn't make the thought of shooting at people any easier to stomach. I've been in my share of fights, but I've never used a knife or a gun in them. I've never wanted to kill anyone, even by accident. Now I have no choice. If I don't shoot a few holes in that car, Dani and I won't make it out of here. I have to risk causing a deadly accident, or that a shot might go wild and kill one of the men in the car.

Good. You should kill them. If you don't, you and Dani will never be safe.

We're never going to be safe anyway. If I kill those men, the people they work for will just hire more. If Dr. Connor was telling the truth and there's no way to reverse the changes to our DNA, Dani and I are going to be on the run or hiding from evil assholes for the rest of our lives.

The thought makes my chest hitch. I'll never sit on that lumpy couch with Trent watching crappy movies again. I'll never convince Traci she isn't as stupid as she thinks she is, that she could pull it together and get her dental assistant's license renewed if she tried. I'll never get to tell either of them thanks for doing what they did—for giving me a home and something that felt a little bit like a family.

Of course, they were my roommates, and occasionally my friends, more than my parents. But we've had some good times mixed in with the bad. We made fun of reality shows together, fried chicken on Saturday nights, spent rainy Sunday afternoons playing cards. We went down to the bar after Trent got off work and shot pool, and headed out to the woods every November to hunt for meat to fill the deep-freeze in the garage…

But now it's time to hunt something a lot more dangerous than a deer. Something I have no doubt is going to fight back.

The road opens up around the next curve, stretching straight for another mile or more, every inch of it as deserted as this narrow highway has been for hours. We aren't going to find a better spot.

"Hold on. I'm going to turn around." Dani braces herself and I brake hard, turning the wheel to the left, sending the car spinning in a circle. Dani sucks in a frightened breath I can barely hear over the squeal of tires.

By the time we grind to a stop in the middle of the road, both of us are breathing faster but we're pointed in the right direction. We're facing the car bearing down on us, waiting for it to make its appearance around the curve. When it does, I'm going to be ready.

I rack the gun, sliding the first bullet into the chamber. I lower the window and lean out, taking aim at the road. I've never shot a semi-automatic before—the only gun I've ever touched is a rifle during deer season—but I'm a pretty good shot. Hopefully good enough to hit the wheels or something else that keeps the car moving, and make sure these guys won't be following us any farther.

If I succeed, maybe Dani won't have to call Rachel out again. Maybe we'll make a clean getaway and start a new life in Canada. Maybe we'll take new names, find a place to stay, pretend to have some absent grown-up looking out for us, and settle down with Rachel and the Thing and live happily ever after.

And maybe the tooth fairy will fly down and pay me for all those teeth she never bothered to snag from under my pillow.

I hear the hissing sound behind me just seconds before the black car zips around the corner. The Thing. It's here. Trouble ahead and behind, and me and Dani stuck in the middle and I don't know what to do.

I hesitate a second too long, hunger and exhaustion and the endless adrenaline of the day finally catching up with me and making me slow, stupid, useless. Before I can decide whether to shoot the car or turn and face the beast, a gunshot cracks through the air. A second later, my hand explodes.

Blood—hot and bright—splatters into my face, across the calm beige of the car door, down onto the pavement where a pale worm of a thing twitches on the ground next to the gun. It takes me a second to realize the worm isn't a worm at all. It's a finger. My finger. Shot right off my body but still moving.

And then the fire blasts the back of my neck, reminding me I have bigger things to worry about than a stupid finger.

Dani screams. I scream louder, a hoarse cry that rips through my chest the same way the pain rips through my body. My nerve endings rage and agony flows up my arm, scalding the skin at my neck. I spin, trying to get a look at the Thing, but there's only fire, red and orange and yellow, eating up Dr. Connor's nice leather seats. The entire back of the car is going up. We have to get out.

Slowly, I become aware of hands tugging at my clothes, pulling me from the driver's seat.

"Come on!" Dani pulls harder. Her eyes squeeze shut and her cheeks flush red. She's already outside, halfway to some sort of safety, but determined to pull danger out with her. "Jesse, come on! Hurry!"

I try to force my legs to lift over the gearshift and step out the door, but my muscles won't cooperate. I can't move, can't think, can only watch open-mouthed and horrified as the Thing slinks up behind Dani.

"Stop! Leave her alone!" I scream, trying to believe words will make a difference. "Go away! Get the fuck out of here!" But the dragon just smiles its bloody smile and bares its sharp teeth. "Run, Dani! The Thing's right there. Behind you!"

"I won't leave you! Come with me!" She grabs my good hand and tugs hard enough to scoot me a few inches further from the flames licking at the back of my seat. But even her super strength isn't super enough to pull two-hundred and twenty-five pounds of dead weight out of a car by one hand.

It's too late anyway. The Thing is so close to her now, there's no way she'll be able to escape. It's going to kill her just to prove there's nothing it can't take away. It'll take the girl I love, and then it will take my life the way it tried to so many times when I was a kid.

In that moment, I wish I'd let it. I wish I'd never lived to put Dani in this kind of danger.

The dragon crouches low, wiggling its haunches. Seconds later, the black car pulls to a stop a few feet behind it. Agent Bullock and the Man in Gray jump out, guns drawn, ensuring that—even if by some miracle Dani and I escape the Thing—there will be no happy ending here today.

I'm not a hero; I'm a dumb kid. Now I'm going to die. And Dani's going to die, too, and it's all my fault. I've as good as murdered her.

"It's right behind me?" she asks. I nod and she squeezes my hand. "Don't give up. You can do this."

I swallow, wanting to tell her that I can't, to warn her to save herself because I'm not nearly as big and bad as people at school always thought. But I feel so weak that I can barely moan, even when the men rush forward and the dragon lifts one clawed hand above Dani's head.

"I love you," she whispers.

She spins so fast that her hair swats my cheek, making it sting, bringing back my awareness of all my other hurts—the short-circuiting nightmare that is my four-fingered hand, the burns on the back of my neck, the screaming protest of my right side as the fire in the back seat gets hotter and hotter, and the stupid knot of hunger at the center of it all that's eating away at my guts and starting to work on my spine. It's ridiculous that I'm still hungry. I'm about to die and watching Dani shove past the dragon just seconds before fire explodes from its mouth.

But the hunger eclipses all the other pain. It's a cold, mean ache at the pit of me that's rendered me useless. There's just no fuel left to burn, with the Thing taking its share.

The thought catches and my thoughts spin around it. Is that why I can't pull it together? Something so stupid? Something so simple?

I force my good hand to reach down to the floor. I fumble across the mat until I find the Power Bar Dani dropped when her dad pulled his gun. I grab it and cram one end into my mouth, holding it with my teeth as I pull the wrapper off with shaking fingers. The second the sugar hits my tongue something inside me revs to life. My jaw works the hard, sticky mess and swallows it down—two bites, three, faster than I've ever eaten anything—and suddenly I can move.

Unfortunately the Thing can still move, too, and it doesn't seem any more inclined to let me live than it did a few seconds ago.

I've barely staggered out of the car when the dragon jumps me. Its claws dig into my bad shoulder and I crumple to the ground. As I fall, I catch a glimpse of Dani and watch helplessly as Agent Bullock's arms close around her from behind. A few feet away, the Man in Gray is already on the ground, his nose gushing red.

Rachel must have gotten him. But Rachel can't be in two places at once and Rachel can't fight the Thing any more than Dani can. Rachel and the dragon may both be imaginary, but they exist in different minds, different worlds. The only person who can stop the monster ripping open my shoulder, making me howl like an animal, is *me*.

"Stop it! Get the hell out of here, you piece of shit!" I scream, using my best "listen up" voice, thinking of all the times that voice has done the job—on the ball field, on the bus at my old school where every trip home was an exercise in survival, downtown after dark in the dangerous places that always felt safer than my own bed.

Safe. Shit! I have to keep *Dani* safe, and the Thing isn't listening to reason.

Guess I'll just have to try brute force. It worked when I was little. The dragon's a hell of a lot stronger now, but so am I and I have something bigger than myself to fight for. I'm not going to fail Dani, not after everything we've been through.

My howl transforms into a battle cry as I grab the Thing by the throat and squeeze with everything in me. I ignore the blood pouring down my left hand. I ignore the fear that zips through me when I hear Dani scream again. I ignore the bit of bone that stabs up from my flesh and the cold puff of my breath and the hot flames that shoot from the dragon's mouth—and I fight.

I punch and kick and hold onto the Thing as it writhes, its reptilian body twisting in ways my muscles can't imagine. It flips me across the ground to slam against the car and back again, over the pavement and off the road into a snow bank where I finally land on top. I lock my legs around its body, holding it down in the snow, thanking God and Coach Clawson that I went out for the wrestling team instead of basketball.

"Jesse! Get down!" Dani shouts.

I duck, slamming my forehead between the Thing's eyes. The satisfying crunch of serpent bone reaches my ears seconds before a gunshot rips through the air. The snow drift behind me takes the bullet intended for my head and sends up a spray of ice and salt.

I turn back to the road. The Man in Gray is up off the ground. Before I can move, he fires again, but this time the shot goes wild. His hand jerks into the air and his legs buckle as some invisible force slams into the back of his knees. He cries out as he hits the pavement, but he lifts his gun again, aiming straight at my chest, my death a certainty in his determined eyes.

The Thing rumbles beneath me. An angry growl simmers in its throat, hums through its scales. I look down to see its red eyes locked on the Man in Gray with a grim determination of their own.

I have a split second to decide: trust the Thing or trust my gut. My gut says the dragon's decided it's in the mood for fresh meat, but if I let it go and it dives for my throat, I'm over and there's no way I'll be able to help Dani.

But if it doesn't...

Dani cries out, a pained sound that makes me angrier than anything I can remember. I don't care if the dragon kills me, as long as I get to destroy the man who is daring to hurt Dani before it does. I roll hard to the left and hurl the Thing at the Man in Gray just as his gun goes off again. This time, he hits a mark. Just not the one he was aiming for.

The Thing absorbs the bullet meant for me and keeps going, landing in a frenzy of sharp claws and snapping teeth. The man screams, an eardrum-shattering wail for mercy that doesn't slow the Thing for a second. The monster shreds him, rips his skin from his bones while he's still alive, turns him into hamburger meat from the stomach down. The pure, bloody violence of it makes Rachel's beating of Dr. Connor look like a skit from *Sesame Street*.

It happens so fast I barely have time to stand up before it's over. The Man in Gray collapses to the ground, bloodied and torn, eyes wide and empty. Dead. In seconds. That's what I can do. That's what this beast inside of me is capable of. I clench my jaw, fighting the urge to be sick. The Thing has been holding back on me, giving me a fighting chance. I realize that now. It never put everything it had into killing me. If it had, I would be dead. I shudder as the dragon rakes its claws through the mess and snaps up chunks of meat. Meat, not human flesh. If I think about that red mess as a person—a person I've killed and that something I've created in my mind is eating—I'm going to go crazy.

I take less than a second to make sure the Thing is distracted and run to Dani, focusing on the fight ahead and how satisfying it will feel to smash my fist into Agent Bullock's face. But Agent Bullock is gone.

I catch sight of him as he slides into the driver's seat

and fires up the black car. Fear has wiped away his smug expression, making him look older and younger at the same time. His slack cheeks seem more wrinkled, but his eyes are baby eyes, saucers full of shattered innocence.

Guess Agent Bullock isn't as big and bad as he thought he was, either.

For a second I think about running after the car, but a glance back at the dragon makes it impossible. It's still eating Bullock's partner. I watch its bloody snout lift into the air as it swallows another chunk whole and know I'd puke if I had more than a Power Bar in my stomach. Let the man go. Let him run back to his bosses and tell them all about this nightmare. Maybe then they'll have the sense to leave us alone.

Bullock pulls out in a squeal of tires, zipping past our car as he—

"Shit!" The car! It's still on fire. It's burning like crazy now, snapping and popping, melting the seats like putty.

I curse again as the black car disappears around a curve in the road, realizing too late why I should have forced myself to pull Bullock out of the driver's seat. We need that car. We're out in the middle of nowhere, miles from civilization, with no transportation, no food, no coats, no shelter, and night is coming on fast. The only good news is that the Thing has vanished now that it's eaten its fill. But already the light has gone pink and gray, the last strands of a winter sunset that will all too quickly fade to cold, black night.

I drive my hands through my hair, wincing when my

fingers brush over shriveled, sticky clumps. The Thing has burned the entire left side of my head. Great. Just what Dani and I need, a new look that will attract attention. I'll have to shave my hair off and start from scratch. But maybe that's a good thing. Maybe being bald will make me look old enough to rent a hotel room if Dani and I can get across the border. Too bad we're really going to have to do it on foot.

Stupid! I'm so stupid!

And you've killed a man. Dead. On the ground. Turn around and get a good look at what happens when you let the Thing take control.

I bite the inside of my lip until I taste blood. I can't turn around. I don't want to see the evidence of my *wrongness*. I can't stand to think that it could have been Dani on the ground if I'd hesitated a second longer, if I hadn't figured out that not eating was hurting instead of helping me control the monster inside of me.

"Jesse?" Dani's voice trembles, thin and breathy, pulling me from my racing thoughts. She wavers on her feet, so pale she's almost glowing.

Another wave of nausea roils through my guts. She must have seen what's left of the man who tried to shoot me. That has to be why she looks like she's about to faint. I've killed someone. Right in front of her.

I hurry across the pavement. My arms go around her waist just as her knees buckle and her head wilts to the side. I help her fold onto the ground, amazed that she can make even passing out look graceful. She's so beautiful, so fragile despite that tough streak inside her. I should have realized that. I should have done a better job of protecting her. If I had, maybe my hands wouldn't be brushing over her stomach and coming away smeared with blood.

If I had, maybe Dani wouldn't be dying in my arms.

Eighteen

Jesse

The Thing got to her. It must have happened when she rushed past it. I saw it take a swipe, but I didn't think it touched her. I didn't realize...I didn't know...and now...

Now...

"Jesse..."

"Just hold still. You're going to be fine." I make the lie sound as much like the truth as I can while taking in Dani's ripped-open body.

I only glance down for a second, but I get an eyeful through the rips in her shirt. Her skin is peeling away from her bones, showing pink and red and shredded muscles and parts of things I don't want to think about, delicate things responsible for keeping Dani alive.

We're both healing crazy fast, but can she survive this kind of damage? I press my hand over the wound, but more red and pink gush out with every breath she takes. Applying pressure isn't going to be enough. She's too messed up.

I have to find help.

Trent's face flashes through my mind, but I push it away. Even if I had a phone and could convince Trent he had to come pick me up in Northern Bum Fuck, he'd never get here in time. Maybe Dani's dad? If I carry her back to the road where we left him he might be able to help her. He's a doctor and way better equipped to deal with this kind of injury than I am.

But he's also an evil bastard. And Agent Bullock knows where Dr. Connor was taking us. Bullock could be on his way to pick him up right now. Maybe they'll even decide to grab some more guns at cabin number thirteen and come back to finish us off.

"Shit," I hiss beneath my breath. I have to get us out of here. Now. But I can't—

"Penny...I don't think...I..." Dani shifts in my arms, licks her lips with a sluggish move of her tongue that scares me. She's fading, dying, while I sit here like a dumb-ass waiting for the bad guys to pull themselves together. "She'll help us."

Her stepmom. The one who used to work for the real FBI. Dr. Connor said that his wife was on the way to a safe house. But he also said that she didn't know anything about what was happening and that he was afraid she might leave him. He obviously lied to us about a few things, but that part I believe. A grown man doesn't cry like a baby for no reason. He was really afraid of losing Penny, and when he talked about starting a new life he said it would be just him and Dani. Like he was assuming Penny wouldn't be able to stomach him now that she knew the truth about his past.

She's probably one of the good guys, and she'll obviously do anything to help Dani. But how to reach her? It's not like we're going to find a pay phone out in the middle of the woods, and Dani's dad threw her cell away. Even if I pick her up and carry her down the road until we get to a place where we can use a phone, there's no guarantee we'll—

Wind whistles through the trees, sending snow gusting into the road. It sticks to the spots of red on the pavement and starts to melt in the blood at the edge of the street. The dead guy. He's been ripped apart, but there's a chance...

Most men carry their cell phones in their pockets.

"What's Penny's number?" I get Dani to repeat it twice so I'll be sure to remember it, just in case she's not awake by the time I get back with the phone.

The thought makes me hug her as tight as I dare before laying her gently on the ground. I kiss her forehead, scared by how cold she feels. "I'll be right back. I'm going to go look for a phone. I'm..." My throat squeezes so tight it's hard to breathe. Looking at Dani's face doesn't make it any easier. I've never felt so much for a person, never known my entire future could live or die if one pair of brown eyes closed forever.

"I'm so sorry." I rub my good hand across my eyes, shocked by the wet heat streaming down my cheeks. I'm crying. For the first time since I was a little kid praying for my mom to come home and tell me that she loved me and make everything okay with a hug and a kiss.

But she hadn't come, and she'd never loved me. Not like this. Not in the way that makes your entire body ache imagining how empty life will be without the person you love. Still, it isn't easy to say the words. I'm afraid. Not afraid of saying it for the first time, just afraid that the first time will be the last.

"I love you." My voice catches, betraying my fear. "Don't die, Dani. Please."

Her hand finds mine. "I won't. Hurry. You're hurt."

I look down. My pointer finger is a stump with a shard of bone peeking out. Dani brushes it lightly with her fingers and her eyebrows draw together. She's the one whose insides are about to spill out and she's worried about *me*. Because she loves me, too.

I can't lose her. I just…can't. I press a quick kiss to lips even colder than her skin, and turn and run for the mess on the side of the road.

Mess. Just a mess. Not a person. Not a person I *killed*.

I keep my eyes firmly above the shredded flesh and do my best not to look into the dead man's eyes. A part of me is tempted to close his lids, but I don't. I can't stand the thought of touching his face. I don't want to touch any part of him, but I make myself throw open his jacket and pick through the inner pockets of his suit coat.

One is shredded and soaked with blood and the other holds a slim wallet with nothing in it but a driver's license, a couple of credit cards, and sixty bucks. I stuff the money in my pocket—Dani and I will need cash—and turn him over. I check what's left of his belt, trying not to puke as his guts spill out the back of him.

Intestines. Those are intestines. I think about the illustrations in my bio book, concentrate on naming all the parts of the body I can remember as I push the slimy stuff out of the way. I find the other half of the belt and track my fingers along the leather. Finally, I find what feels like a cell phone case and I pull it—dripping with gore—from the mess.

I almost puke for real then, but I don't. I hold it in, clamp my lips together and suck my stomach in tight as I wipe off the blood and unsnap the leather case. The phone inside is wet, but not too wet. The case protected it from the worst of the…

I swallow. Hopefully it will still work, hopefully I'll have bars, hopefully Dani's stepmom will answer and make it here in time.

Hope, hope, hope, pray, pray, pray.

I flick the phone open and watch the screen turn green, hoping and praying some more that the one tiny block on the upper left hand side is enough of a signal to reach Penny.

My thumbs jab at the buttons and the call connects and suddenly I'm so aware of the chill in the air and the fire in my hand and the phantom feel of that missing finger and the blood soaking through my jeans and the hard

ground beneath my knees. Three seconds, four, and somewhere in the darkening forest a crow calls again and again,
and still there's no answer on the end of the line. My hands
shake so hard I'm afraid I'll drop the phone. Deep inside, a
cold, lonely, stillness spreads beneath my skin.

And then—faint and scratchy—a voice says "hello."
My heart slams in my chest. I turn back to Dani. I want
her to know that her stepmom has picked up, I want—

I choke on the words rising in my mouth. Dani's eyes
are closed and the hand she was pressing to her middle
has slipped to the ground. She lies still on the asphalt, her
fingers curled the softest bit. She looks like she's sleeping,
but I know she's unconscious.

Or dead.

"Hello? Who is this?" Penny's voice comes again. She
sounds scared, stuffy, like she's been crying and couldn't
stop before she answered the phone. I try to say something, to answer her question, but there's a lump in my
throat that won't let the words come out. "Hello? Dani? Is
this you? Honey?"

Dani. Adrenaline shoots through my body. "No, this
is Jesse. I'm with Dani, but she's hurt, maybe even dying."
I try to catch my breath, but can't and continue in a whisper. "I don't know what to do."

"Oh my God," Penny says. "Where are you, Jesse?
Can you call an ambulance, are you—"

"No, we're almost to Canada. We're stuck on the side
of the road." I tell her the highway name and the mile

marker, as close as I can remember. "Dr. Connor was taking us to a cabin to meet some people, but he…"

How to tell her that her husband tried to kill me? How to tell her that terrorists want to kidnap me and Dani? How to tell her that the entire world has gone crazy and make her believe it enough to help me keep Dani safe? I have no idea. Thank God I don't have to explain.

"Don't worry, Jesse. I'm getting in the car right now." I hear a door slam and the quality of her voice changes. "I'm not far from you. Maybe ten or fifteen minutes."

Thank God. The news makes me shudder and a sob of relief slip from my lips.

"Barrett told me I was supposed to meet him and Dani at a hunting lodge near the border. He said we'd be entering the witness protection program because of his work, but I called one of my old friends from the FBI on the way up here. No one in the witness protection program ever contacted Barrett, and he's being investigated for…several things." She pauses, and I know I'm supposed to speak, but it's still so hard. "Jesse, are you there?"

"I'm here." I let out a sigh that sounds as broken as I feel. "Just…hurry. If you can. There were some men here with guns. One of them might be back soon and Dani's eyes are closed and I don't know…I don't know what to do."

"Oh no. Was she shot? Is she—"

"No. She was cut, but it's bad."

"But there were people there with guns?" Penny asks, talking slowly and carefully like she's not sure I'm in my right mind. Maybe she's right. Maybe I'm not. "Are you two safe for a few more minutes? Until I get there? Is there anywhere you can hide or—"

"I think we're okay for a few more minutes. But the car is on fire. And I'm…I'm not good." I'm worse than not good. I'm numb all over and the cold just keeps getting colder. The sight of Dani lying there so still has accomplished what a day filled with terror hasn't. I'm losing it.

Going…going…

"Okay. Just stay away from the car and keep Dani warm. It's freezing out there and she could go into shock. Are you in another car? Can you turn on the heat?"

"No, but I'll…" I stagger to my feet and stumble a few wooden steps before collapsing by Dani's side. She's breathing, slow and shallow, but steady. I sob again as I strip off my sweater and lay it over her. I take her limp hand in my whole one and pray that Penny will get here fast.

"Jesse? Can you hear me?"

"Dani's alive," I say, finding it harder and harder to form words. "I covered her with my sweater."

"Okay. Good job. Just hold on, honey," she says, such genuine warmth in her voice that I feel that lump rise in my throat again. "You're going to be fine. Everything is going to be okay."

The lump becomes another sob and more stupid tears, but I can't seem to stop them. I can't be strong anymore. Penny's kindness—and how damned relieved I am to hear somebody tell me everything is going to be okay—slams the ugly truth home with a vengeance.

I'm not a grown-up; I can't handle this. I'm seventeen years old and the only real friend I've ever had might be dying on the ground next to me and I'm helpless. I've proved I can destroy things, kill people, but I can't heal Dani. I can't do anything but hold her hand and wish for her life harder than I've ever wished for anything.

Nineteen

Jesse

I shrink inside myself. Movement becomes impossible. The weight of fear crushes my chest. I can't think. Can't speak. I can't respond when Penny tells me she can see me, and that she'll be here any second. I don't even look up when a car roars in from the north and comes to a rubber-squealing stop a dozen yards away. If it's one of the bad guys, let them have me. If it's Penny, she'll—

Suddenly, Penny's next to me, her hand gentle on my back. She tells me I "did a good job" and then turns her full attention to her stepdaughter. She kneels by Dani's shoulders, cups Dani's cheek for a second before lifting the sweater covering her stomach and letting it fall back into place with a gasp. "What happened? Was it an animal?"

"No, it was a…some kind of knife." Better to keep things vague. Now isn't the time to start talking about imaginary enemies, altered DNA, and the psychic manifestations of my overactive immune system.

"God. She's just a kid. I don't…" Penny presses the

back of her shaking hand to her lips before going back in, this time lifting the sweater for several seconds, pulling at the torn sweatshirt, revealing the gashes in Dani's skin.

The four scratches are an ugly red, but not nearly as big as they were a few minutes ago. The open wounds have closed and there's nothing spilling out. She's healing. She's going to be okay. My eyes flick to her face and I sigh again, this time in relief. A flush of pink is returning to her cheeks.

"I should call 911," Penny says. "I didn't see a town big enough for a hospital for miles on this side, but maybe I missed something."

"No, she's better. I think she's going to be okay, at least to ride in the car for a while. We should get farther away before we stop," I say, hoping Penny will believe me. "A few minutes ago I could see…stuff under the skin. She's already better."

Penny shoots me a strange look. "Are you sure? In just a few—"

"I can try to explain, but we should drive while I do it." I kneel by Dani and slide my arms under her knees and shoulders. Penny stops me with a hand on my arm.

"Jesse, I really don't think we should move her. She's lost a lot of blood and could have internal injuries. We don't know if it's okay to—"

"I know she's *not* going to be okay if we're still here when the guys with guns come back. They already shot at us twice." I don't tell her about the bullet in my shoulder, I don't want to make her worry about having to stop somewhere because of me. Slowly, I inch the hand with the missing finger behind Dani's leg.

Penny pales before nodding slowly. "Okay, but be as gentle as you can. We'll lie her down in the back seat."

I follow Penny to her car—a navy BMW parked in the middle of the road, the driver's door still hanging open, giving testimony to how fast she'd rushed to Dani's side. Penny seems to love her stepdaughter. Now if only I can convince her that the best way to show it is for her to contact her friends in the FBI and start making that witness protection program lie a reality.

But is the FBI really safe? Won't they find out the truth about the Dream Project kids sooner or later? Maybe they already know. Maybe Dr. Connor wasn't lying about working on classified projects for the feds.

I shut the inner voice down as I carry Dani into the back seat and get her settled—long legs curled on one side and the rest of her spilling into my lap. I'll worry about whether or not the FBI is safe later. First we have to get out of here and get Dani to a hospital. Once I'm positive she's going to be okay, maybe I'll be able to start thinking straight again.

"I'm going to go north for a few minutes and catch the main highway south," Penny says. "I think the way I came is safe. I didn't see anyone coming or going." She grabs a red scarf and a fatter blue one from the passenger's seat and turns to press them into my hand. "Here. Wrap one of these around your neck and one around Dani's. I know it's not much, but it will help you warm up."

I don't feel cold anymore, but I do what she says. I wrap the soft blue scarf around my neck with clumsy fingers and then ease the red one around Dani's throat. Penny starts the car and turns around, heading back the way she came. I breathe easier with every foot she puts between us and the mess on the side of the road. Thank God she didn't notice the dead man. I don't know what I would have told her.

"Where's Barrett?" Penny asks, concern for her husband in her voice. Even if she's planning to leave him, it seems like she still cares. "Is he okay?"

Is he okay? I don't know and it seems wrong to lie. So I don't.

I tell her everything, starting with what Dani and I found out on our own and adding all the things Dr. Connor explained. I tell her about her brother trying to kidnap us, the attacks by the things in our heads, the terrorist group with their guns, and our super-healing powers. The only thing I leave out is the most important thing—that Dani, at least, has learned to control her overactive imagination and turn it into a weapon. It seems best to keep that a secret right now. We don't want to make anyone afraid of us. I can see only one way that would end. Badly.

Penny takes it all in without saying much. Afterward, she drives in silence for what seems like forever before she finally responds. "I think we need to talk about this more when Dani's awake."

"But it's true," I say. "I promise it is. Dani will tell you the same thing."

"I believe you. Barrett told me this afternoon that he was part of some very…unethical experiments." Her tone turns cold. Whether she still loves her husband or not, she seems appropriately disgusted by what he did. "But I…I just want to wait until Dani's awake, okay? I need to hear her side of things before we make any big decisions."

She doesn't believe me. It's what I expected, but still…it hurts. And it scares the hell out of me. If she refuses to believe me, then Dani and I are still in danger. We can't go back to Madisonville. Not ever. And Penny will—

"But I don't think it's a good idea to go back home tonight," she says. "We don't want to be anyplace that Barrett or these people might think to look for us until we make sure you and Dani are safe. I'm going to call one of my old work friends. He might be able to help us find a place to stay for a few days. We'll call your parents and let them know what's going on as soon as we know where we're headed."

My shoulders ease away from my neck as she slips in her ear piece and dials. It isn't a long-term solution, but it's enough. And maybe Dani can convince Penny I'm telling the truth.

I glance down at her. She's definitely just sleeping.

Her breath is long and even and her eyelids flutter when I brush a piece of hair from her cheek. Her impossibly soft hair. I keep my fingers where they are, smoothing through her tangles as I listen to Penny's end of a conversation.

She tells some guy named Gerard about the investigation into her husband's work and North Corp. She says she doesn't know who she can trust anymore, and that she needs a safe place to keep two teenagers she believes are in danger until she can figure it out. She doesn't say anything about imaginary enemies or psychic powers, but she doesn't seem so worried anymore about getting Dani to a doctor, either. She merges onto the freeway headed south and zips through the first big town without bothering to exit and search for a hospital.

Maybe she believes more of my story than she's letting on. Or maybe she's too scared to stop. I'm just glad she hasn't noticed my missing finger or I'm pretty sure we'd be on our way to the nearest emergency room. There are time limits for things like reattaching missing digits.

No, not missing. Gone. That finger is gone. Forever. It's going to rot on the side of the road. By spring it will be nothing but bone. Still, I can't bring myself to care that much. It's only a finger. I'm still alive. Not like that man I killed, the man I murdered, shredded like some kind of animal.

"Okay, we've got a destination." Penny pulls me from my thoughts before they can eat me alive. "My old supervisor is a really good guy. I trust him. He has a place we can stay in the city, not too far from Times Square. He's going to have a doctor meet us there, but I can pull over on the way if we have to. Just keep an eye on Dani and make sure she—"

"I'm fine." Dani is still scary pale and she doesn't try to sit up or move her head from my lap, but she's awake. Awake! I squeeze her shoulder, so grateful to see her eyes open that my arm shakes.

"Where are we?" she asks.

"In Penny's car," I say. "She was close by. She came to get us."

"I'm here, Dani." Penny glances over her shoulder. Relief softens her face when her stepdaughter lifts a weak hand in salute. "We're on our way to the city. I'm going to make sure you and Jesse are safe."

"What happened? What did Dad—"

Penny tells her what happened and where we're going. Dani tells her the same story I told, but Penny still seems doubtful. Even when Dani sits up and lifts her shirt, showing her stepmom her miraculously healed skinned, Penny doesn't seem to be buying.

"I'm just so glad you're okay," Penny says. "But I still want the doctor to check you out when we get to the apartment. We can talk more about all of this, and your dad, and…everything else *after* I'm sure you don't need to go to a hospital."

Dani sighs and runs careful fingers over my hurt hand. Unfortunately, it *hasn't* healed like magic. The skin has knit together and it doesn't hurt anymore, but there's still no finger there. Guess even superheroes have their limitations. My stomach growls, and dread creeps into the cozy warmth of the back seat.

Speaking of limitations…

"Can we pull over and get something to eat?" I ask. "Dani and I haven't had much to eat all day." On the run for our lives or not, we need food. I have to be fueled up and ready to fight if the Thing comes back. I have to make sure I have enough strength to keep it from hurting anyone ever again.

"Sure." Penny glances in the rearview mirror. "I haven't noticed anyone following us. I'll take the next exit and we can get something for the road." She turns on her blinker and eases off the highway, toward a rash of brightly lit fast food restaurants. "Cheeseburgers and fries okay? It looks like that's all they've got, and it will probably be quick."

"That's fine." It's better than fine. My mouth is watering already. I can't believe I'm so hungry, but I am. Apparently my gut isn't bothered by the images of the dead man that keep flashing behind my eyes. At least not as bothered as my brain.

Penny pulls into the lot of the closest burger joint— a grungy-looking place called the Burger Giant with a cow wearing angel wings spinning on top of its roof— and parks a few spots down from the door. "I've got your meter and shots in my purse, Dani." She fishes out her wallet and passes the rest of her purse over the seat. "Why don't you check your sugar while I run in and get you guys some cheeseburgers. I don't want anyone to see either of you. Just in case."

"Okay." Dani starts to unwrap her scarf, but Penny stops her with a hand on her knee.

"Can you both leave your scarves on? I know I'm a worry wart, but I don't want you to go into shock and keeping warm is important. I'd stop and get you coats, but I don't—"

"It's fine, Penny. Don't worry about it. We'll keep the scarves on." Dani puts her hand on her stepmom's. "Thanks for worrying about us. And thank you for…everything else. I…I really…I love you. I didn't realize how much until today. I'm so sorry that I didn't—"

"Oh, honey. You don't have to thank me or apologize for anything. I love you, too." Tears fill Penny's eyes. She pulls her fingers from beneath Dani's to swipe them away. "No matter what happens, I'm on your side. Remember that, okay?"

"Okay." Dani sniffs and dabs her eyes with the back of her hand.

"Just check your sugar and I'll be right back with cheeseburgers and fries and whatever else looks good." Penny reaches for the door. "Lock the doors behind me and honk the horn if you see anything that scares you."

Dani nods and makes a show of looking into Penny's purse, but stops as soon as her stepmom disappears through the brightly lit door. She sighs. "I really do love her."

"I can tell."

"But she's never going to believe that I don't need shots anymore."

"Maybe she will. Maybe she just needs some time." I scan the parking lot out of habit, some part of my brain not quite ready to believe we're safe. "At least she's not taking us back to Madisonville."

Dani finds my hand again. "If she were, we'd have to leave." She threads her fingers through mine and squeezes tight. "Maybe we should leave anyway."

My growling stomach twists into a knot. "Why? Don't you trust her?"

"No, I do. Completely. But what about..." Dani stares at the floorboards. "I just don't want her to get hurt. I couldn't live with myself if we hurt her."

Not *we*. *Me*. I'm the one who doesn't have control. I'm the one who killed a man.

I want to tell her that everything is going to be okay, but she's right. Penny doesn't know what she's risking by helping us. Her connections at the FBI might keep us safe for a little while, but sooner or later the Thing will be back and no one will be safe.

I pull my hand from hers. "I'll leave. You stay with Penny."

"No." Dani meets my eyes with a stubborn look that scares me. "I won't leave you. We're staying together."

"Dani...that man is dead. And you..." I swallow, hating to speak the words but knowing I have to. "I almost killed you, too."

"But you didn't, and you got control."

I shake my head. "No, I didn't. That was just dumb luck. I can't promise that I'll be able to make the dragon listen again. And next time it could do to you what it did to him. You have to let me—"

"No. We're staying together. We'll call Penny as soon as we're safe." Dani paws through Penny's purse, finds a few loose bills, and stuffs them in her pocket before shoving the purse onto the floor. "Come on, we—"

"It ate him, Dani. In chunks." I feel even sicker, but I'll say whatever it takes to get through to her. She has to let me go and promise she'll never come looking for me. "I can't risk that happening to you. Please don't make me."

Dani turns to me. I expect more words, but she surprises me with a kiss. Her mouth lingers on mine just long enough to make my pulse race before she pulls back to whisper against my lips. "It's my life to risk. And I think you're worth it."

"I'm not."

"You are to me." She kisses me again and I lose my will to fight. If our positions were reversed, I would handcuff myself to her side and throw away the key before I'd let her fight her invisible demons, and the bad guys who are after us, on her own.

My arms go around her and I pull her close, but only for a second. As good as she feels, there's no time. If we're going, we've got to go. Now. "Penny will be back soon."

Dani nods. "Okay. Just let me pop the trunk. I bet she packed me a suitcase before she left home. If I have clothes, it will be one less thing to buy." She leans over the seat and hits a button. The trunk thunks open behind us and Dani hurries out of the car. I follow, scooting across the seat.

She's already lifting the trunk when my feet hit the pavement and the feeling that something's wrong shivers across my skin, carried on a blast of cold night air. Dani's leaning over to grab her suitcase—her back still turned to the mostly deserted parking lot—when I realize where the bad feeling is coming from.

A gray van slides into a space a dozen feet away and two men and a woman, all in jeans and black coats, step out. The men wear sunglasses even though the sun went down an hour ago, and the woman's long red hair is pulled back into a tight ponytail. Even before they reach into their coats and pull out their guns, I know they're here for us. They're too sleek for this tiny upstate town, and no woman wears her hair like that unless she's getting ready for some serious physical activity.

Like chasing down superhuman kids and shoving them into the back of her van.

"Dani!" I reach for her and she dives into my arms. I catch her and pull her behind the car just as the red-headed woman fires. Electricity arcs through the air, hitting the trunk where Dani was standing a second ago.

"Come on, this way." I grab her arm and rush for the

door of the Burger Giant. I hate to put Penny and the few other people inside in danger, but it's the only way we'll have a chance. The parking lot backs onto an open field and the grocery store next door is closed. There's nowhere else to run, and there's at least a chance the three people behind us will be unwilling—or unable—to Taser a dozen people before Dani and I figure out another way to escape.

Dani is stumbling along behind me, but before we round the front of the car, Penny pushes through the restaurant door. She's clutching a fat brown bag in one hand and a tray of drinks in the other, but she doesn't keep hold of them for long. Her eyes skim over me and Dani, taking in our frightened faces, before finding the people behind us. The bag falls. The drinks go a second later as she shoves her hand into her puffy white coat and pulls out a gun.

A real gun. Just like the one Dr. Connor almost killed me with.

"Get back!" she shouts, bracing the weapon with her other hand. She steps over the spilled drinks without taking her attention from the three people standing in the middle of the parking lot. I risk a glance over at the car, surprised to see the two men backing away. The redhead, however, turns her gun to the sky but holds her ground.

"We're here on orders, Penny. We're supposed to take Jesse and Dani with us."

Penny sucks in a breath. "Gerard called you?"

"He just wants them to be safe. We all want them safe."

Penny shakes her head. "No. You can't take them, Mara. I won't let you. You were there with me. You know what they're doing to the others."

The redhead—Mara—sighs. "I know. But what other choice do we have?"

"We have the choice to treat these kids with respect and compassion," Penny says, her voice breaking. "They've already been through hell and—"

"And they can kill people. They're deadly, Penny, and nothing you wrap around their neck is going to hold the things in their heads off for long," Mara says.

I reach for the scarf at my throat and rub the perfectly normal-feeling yarn between my fingers. What is this thing? For a second I consider ripping it off, but I stop myself. Penny's lied like everyone else, but at least she seems to be on our side.

"You're risking your life," Mara says, "and *their* lives if you don't—"

"Don't listen to her, Penny." Dani has recovered from the shock of learning that her stepmom knows the bad guys by name a hell of a lot faster than I have. "We can control the manifestations. We won't hurt you."

Penny shoots Dani a lightning-quick look of gratitude. "Please, Mara," she says, turning her attention back to the redhead, who has inched closer until she and Penny stand at opposite ends of Penny's BMW. "Just let us go. I'll find a place to hide and you can say we never saw each other tonight."

Mara shifts her focus and I find myself staring into her eyes. She's the one holding the Taser, but I can see how scared she is. She doesn't want to force me and Dani into her van. She knows what we're capable of.

"Two hours," she whispers, tucking her stun gun back into her coat. A few feet behind her, the two men turn and walk back to the van. "I'll give you two hours. Then I'll call Gerard and tell him we saw you pulling through the border crossing into Canada. I suggest you head southwest."

Penny's gun arm shakes before falling to her side. "Thank you." She waves to Dani and me with her other hand. "Get in the car, guys. Hurry." I hesitate, but only for a second. I don't trust Penny, but right now she's all we've got.

Still, as I duck into the car behind Dani, I wonder if I'm making the right choice. Am I going to look back on this moment and wish I'd made another decision? Even if it seems like a stupid one right now?

"It's going to be okay," Dani whispers as Penny pulls out of the parking lot and down the ramp heading south on the freeway. "We're together. We'll figure this out. We'll make sure Penny's safe. It'll be okay."

She's right. The only way I'll ever be "okay" is with her. No matter where this ride ends, I'll never regret staying with Dani.

But that doesn't mean I have to go quietly.

I move so fast Penny barely has time to flinch before the gun fisted in her hand is in mine.

"What are—"

"Keep your hands on the wheel," I say. I press the barrel to the base of her skull. "And start talking."

"Jesse, put the gun down!" Dani pulls at my arm, but I hold my position.

"Don't worry. I'm not going to shoot her…" I pause, thumbing off the safety with a soft click. "As long as she tells the truth."

I wouldn't shoot her if she told me the sky was purple with green spots, but Penny can't know that. Hopefully my scary voice can still work a little magic. If we don't find out what's really happening soon, I feel like I'm going to lose my mind.

"Jesse, I don't—"

"I've been working for the FBI." Penny interrupts before Dani can complete her protest. "Before he passed away, my father and I were working a surveillance mission, monitoring the scientists involved in the Dream Project. The experiment was originally funded by the government, but it isn't supported anymore, and the FBI wanted to make sure the project stayed dead—that none of the people involved continued their work or told anyone what they'd been part of. So undercover surveillance teams were put on all five original members of the project. My marriage to Dani's father was part of that surveillance."

"What?" Dani falls back into her seat, looking less like she wants to grab the gun from my hand. "But…you've been together almost six years."

"I know." Penny flips the left turn signal and pulls out into the other lane, passing a long row of semi trucks. "I'm sorry. I couldn't tell you the truth, but I really...I meant what I said in the parking lot. I care about you so much. I consider you family, and I'll do whatever it takes to keep you safe."

"Even from the FBI?" I ask, keeping the gun where it is.

"I think you saw that for yourself." Penny sounds awfully reasonable for a woman with a gun pointed at her head. But then, if she's telling the truth, she's an FBI agent and probably trained not to freak out at times like this. "Mara and I work together...used to work together," she says. "We were some of the last agents to learn that the Dream Project isn't so dead after all. For several years now, the government has been rounding up the kids. We were debriefed a couple of weeks ago, and taken to visit the facility where the FBI is keeping them." Penny's hands tighten on the wheel. "That's when I knew I had to find a way to stop the project. Dani wasn't scheduled to be reactivated until she was seventeen, so I thought I had some time, but..."

"But someone decided to step up the schedule." Dani's voice is high-pitched, wobbly, as if she can't decide whether to laugh or cry.

"I'm not sure," Penny whispers. "Vince is working for someone who wants Barrett's research on the Dream Project. It could be a foreign government or a terrorist organization, but he said..."

"He said what?" Dani demands.

"He said it was one of our dad's old friends from the FBI who hired him to get you on the bus to New York City. I told him he was a liar. That's when he hit me," she says. "But a few minutes after you and Jesse left the house, I got a call from my supervisor. He said a team had already collected four of the kids they were hoping to reactivate from the wreck, but that I should watch for you two and bring you in. I didn't know Jesse was part of this until that phone call, and…I…I don't know how the FBI could have known about the wreck in time to pick up the other kids unless…"

"Unless the FBI planned it," Dani says.

"Right." Penny pulls back into the right lane, but has to slide into the left again almost immediately. The line of semi trucks seems to stretch on forever. "They also knew that you and Jesse were experiencing the psychic manifestations again. That's why they gave me the scarves," she says. "They're threaded with copper wire and charged with a mild electrical current. The scientists working on the Vision Project say they help prevent the manifestations."

"The Vision Project," Dani echoes.

"That's what the FBI is calling the experiment this time around."

We're quiet for a few minutes. I catch Dani tugging her scarf off and fight the urge to pull mine off, too. But if it's really helping to keep the Thing away, I can't risk removing it no matter how trapped it's making me feel.

"I saw some of what they're doing when I visited the facility," Penny continues. "The kids who cooperate in the experiments are isolated in their rooms. The ones who don't cooperate are drugged. And that's not even the worst of it."

"What's the worst of it?" I remind her there's a gun to her head with a nudge of my wrist.

"Electroshock therapy, experiments with different versions of the original formula, infecting healthy kids with diseases to see what they're capable of fighting off." The horror in Penny's voice makes me feel stupid. And cruel. I ease the gun away, but she keeps talking. "I think they're performing surgeries, too. I wasn't allowed into that part of the facility, but my tour leader mentioned something about the doctors having success with an implant." She shakes her head. "And they're doing all of this without the permission of the kids or their parents."

She pauses, wipes at her cheek. I realize that she's crying and feel even worse. "Most of the parents think their children are missing. Or dead. The people on the project justify what they're doing by saying they have no choice. They say the kids who were part of this experiment are too dangerous to be allowed basic human rights." She accelerates, pulling past an oversized U-Haul. One of the semis pulls out of line to ride our ass, its headlights glaring in the rearview mirror. "I can't imagine why they let me in the door to that place. They had to know I'd never support something like this."

"I'm sorry, Penny," Dani says. "Thank you for...I mean...I don't know what to say. This has been your whole life."

"Not my whole life. Just seven years." She smiles, a sad smile that makes her look older. "It was worth it to me. I was part of a different North Corp trial years ago, when I was a teenager. The drug was supposed to treat insomnia, but we found out later that it was one of the experimental meds. It's the reason I can't have children."

"I'm so sorry," Dani says.

Penny glances over her shoulder. "Don't be. It could be worse, right?" The words are barely out of her mouth when the semi roaring behind us rams into the back of the car, sending Dani and me slamming into the seats.

"Buckle up and hold on!" Penny stomps the accelerator to the floor. The BMW leaps forward as Dani and I pull on our seat belts.

After the initial burst of speed, the zip from sixty to one hundred is smooth, flawless. We hit the next uphill stretch going one hundred and ten and soon we're leaving the semi in the dust as it begins to labor up the hill. No matter what kind of engine the bad guys have in that thing, it's not going to be able to catch us now.

But if there are already people tailing us, then Penny's old work buddy must have broken her promise. Mara must have told her boss which direction we're *really* heading. We have to get off the highway.

I lean forward, but there's no time to tell Penny what I think we should do. The white car comes out of nowhere, sliding from between two semis and into our lane less than a hundred feet ahead of the speeding BMW. Penny is going way too fast to stop in time. I know we're fucked even before the white car's brake lights blaze and I realize the person driving is one of them.

Penny slams on the brakes, but it's too late. We're already on top of those cherry red lights that glow just like my dragon's eyes. I reach for Dani, but before I can touch her, the cars collide. Metal screams and my seat belt bites at my shoulder, trying to cut me in half. My chin snaps to my chest, my spine screams, and then there is glass and heat and pain. The rear end of the car lifts into the air while the front is eaten alive by the impact.

I'm conscious long enough to watch Penny be crushed between the steering wheel and her seat and then the night goes black and I am gone.

Twenty

Dani, Six months later

A cool wind rushes in from the ocean and whispers across our sun-warmed skin, swirling the scent of coconut oil and sunscreen into the air. A few feet away, a swimming pool of still blue water beckons, and all around our private patio tropical plants explode into bloom, bending and bobbing with the weight of their heavy fruit. Sometimes we eat the mangoes and bananas right off the trees. Sometimes, like now, we lie quietly and wait for the tiny monkeys who live nearby to creep in and steal a treat.

During our first weeks on the island, we were too frightened to appreciate our neighbors; by our third month, we took pictures of the mamas with their babies clinging to their fur, and now Jesse and I just sit and watch the monkeys jump from branch to branch. We stare into their strangely human eyes and count the number of rings on their tails and laugh at the perfect, tiny fingers on their hands. We're finally starting to feel safe, finally daring to believe that this new life is more than an intermission before another horror-filled act begins.

There was a time when I wouldn't have appreciated a miracle like this new beginning, but I do now.

Even if I have to spend the rest of my life looking over my shoulder, even if I'll never grow up to become a professional dancer or see my mother or father or home again, I have the sense to be grateful. Sometimes I'm even happy.

"I love you," Jesse whispers, his thumb tracing slow, lazy circles on the top of my hand.

I smile. "I love you, too."

"I think Penny's asleep." He nods to where Penny lies on a lounge chair in the shade on the other side of the pool. He carried her there this morning and we served her breakfast while she watched the tide move out. She's getting better at finding her way around in her wheelchair, but she still feels most comfortable lying down.

The crash shattered so many bones in her legs that they're still in braces six months later and probably always will be. But right now she's asleep with a smile on her face. I'm glad. I hope this island will continue to be a place of peace and healing for her and that some day she'll walk again. No matter how gloomy the predictions of her doctors, it's not hard to imagine a miracle happening at this cottage by the shore. It's so beautiful here, so perfect.

Sometimes it's hard to believe it's even real.

Wake up, asshole. You . . . and . . . always were a dumbass. Rachel's mean, squeaky voice drifts through my head as it does from time to time, but she doesn't appear. She hasn't shown up in real life since the night of the crash. Jesse thinks that second accident must have done something to us, altered our brain function in some way. He doesn't see the Thing anymore, either.

If only the people hunting us knew that we were broken, that there's no longer anything special about me and Jesse. Maybe then they'd give up and we could go home.

You…are… Wake up! Rachel's voice becomes a scream of frustration. I wince and my shoulders hunch around my ears. My heart begins to beat faster and that old, familiar anxiety thrums faintly in my veins.

Something's wrong, something I can't quite put my finger on…

"You okay?" Jesse's knuckles brush along my cheek.

"Rachel's talking again."

"Tell her to shut up," he says. "I hate seeing that look on your face."

"I'll be fine."

"Will you?" His forehead wrinkles and fear flickers in his eyes. "Will I?"

I sit up and scoot onto his lounge chair, wrapping him in my arms and holding tight. "We'll be fine. We're safe now."

"I know." His arms come around me. They're warm, but not as warm as they should be after hours lying in the sun. Jesse says he feels cold a lot, despite the fact that the temperature rarely falls below seventy degrees on the island. "But doesn't it feel like…"

"Like what?"

"Like…" He pulls back, squints as if he's trying to see through fog. "I don't know, but sometimes it's hard to believe this is place is real."

I shiver. I was just thinking the same thing, but that doesn't make it any less crazy. "You feel pretty real to me." I kiss his bare shoulder, smell the sunscreen he put on and a hint of his Jesse smell. But only a hint. It's not as strong as it should be when he's this close. It's…strange.

He hugs me closer. "You do, too, but…I don't know."

"What don't you know?"

"Well, it's…like, I remember feeding Penny this morning, and I remember picking bananas, but I don't remember the last time I ate. Why can't I remember something like that?"

My stomach clenches at the mention of food, but I'm not hungry. I rarely feel hungry here, and I can't remember the last time I ate, either. "We had to have had breakfast. Or at least dinner last night."

Jesse shakes his head. "I don't remember last night. I don't remember going to bed. I never do, and I know I should remember going to sleep across the hall every night when I'd rather be in your room," he says.

His words would make me blush if I weren't also finding it impossible to remember what I'd done last night. What time had I gone to sleep? Had we watched television before we went to bed? Does the cottage even have a television? A second ago, I would have sworn it does, but when I try to focus on the details of our new home, the edges of my memory get blurry.

"You're right," I say, my heart speeding again. "I...I can't remember last night, or this morning before we brought Penny breakfast. What time did we wake up?"

"I don't remember. I only remember lying by the pool and I...have we even gone swimming?" His eyes squeeze shut and his free hand pinches the bridge of his nose.

"Are you okay?"

"I'm losing it...I can't concentrate." He groans and pulls his other hand from around my waist as he rolls onto his side.

I touch his back, feel him shudder beneath my fingers and know I should be worried. But I'm not. I'm starting to feel strangely peaceful again. The soft shush of the waves and the gentle warmth of the sun are working their magic. It's impossible to worry here. No matter what Jesse thinks, no matter how upset he is right now, everything will be okay.

Wake up! Wake... Rachel's voice is muffled now. Soon it will grow so faint I won't be able hear her anymore. Then I can lie back down beside Jesse and take a nap in the sun. We'll both feel better after a nap, and when we wake up we can get Penny and go up to the house and make something to eat. I'll even write down what we have for dinner so that Jesse and I can remember it later and laugh about how forgetful we're becoming.

"Have we ever gone swimming, Dani?" Jesse asks, his voice thick. He sounds like he's about to cry and a sliver of concern pricks at my calm.

"Don't cry, Jesse. I love you. Everything's going to be okay. We're together."

"I don't think we are." He chokes on his next breath and his voice becomes a sob. "I just want to know if we've ever gone swimming!"

Worry for him cuts through my foggy peace like cold air let into an over-warm room. I pull in a breath and look at the pool. It's only five feet from our chairs and as blue and clear and tempting as ever, but I can't remember jumping into the water. I can't remember it closing over my head, soaking into my hair, washing me clean.

I've never been in that pool; I'm suddenly sure of it. And I'm just as sure that I have to get in. Immediately.

I stagger to my feet, lean over to grab Jesse's hand, and haul him up to sit in his chair. My legs feel like hollow reeds that won't bend without breaking, my pulse races like I've danced the entire *Waltz of the Flowers* instead of just gone from sitting to standing, and my mouth is full of ashes. The air tastes burnt, sooty, wrong.

"Come on." I fight the dragging feeling sucking on my arms and legs, demanding that I lie down and go to sleep. "The water. In...the water."

I see the spark of understanding in Jesse's eyes, but he doesn't say anything. His jaw is slack and his lips hang loose, as if he's lost control of his facial muscles. Still, he manages to lurch to his feet and take a few wobbly steps before falling to his knees. I crash to the ground beside him, but the concrete doesn't bruise me. I don't feel the pain, only the stubborn warmth of the sun and the equally stubborn whoosh of the breeze. My eyelids are heavy, so heavy it seems impossible to keep my eyes open.

But the water is so close. If we can just get to the water…

"Come…" I claw at Jesse's hand, urging him to crawl along beside me. He manages to move one hand forward and then the other, but collapses at the water's edge. I grab his shoulder and shake him. A part of me screams that it's insane to try to force a person who can't even walk into a pool of water. He'll drown. I'll kill him.

Another part of me insists that the water is the only way to save Jesse's life.

"Cuh…cuh…" I can't form words anymore. My face feels puffy and loose, my tongue slips from between my teeth. Even if I can struggle those last few inches and fall into the pool, I'll never be able to swim. This is suicide.

Right. Suicide. It's Rachel's voice again, faint but clear enough for me to understand. *That's what they said when you jumped off the roof.*

But I didn't jump off the roof. Rachel tricked me.

I'm not the only one with tricks. Get in the water. Wake up!

"Go." Jesse points to the pool, obviously unable to move any other part of him. But that small gesture is enough to send adrenaline surging into my veins.

My eyelids fly up, my lungs fill with air. He's pointing with his left hand. His left hand with all four fingers and thumb still healthy and attached. But I was there when he lost one of those fingers. I held his bloody hand in the car. I remember how sick it made me to know that we'd left a piece of him behind. If circumstances had been different, we might have been able to get him to a hospital and have the finger reattached, but we hadn't. We'd crashed into the white car and just barely escaped with our lives.

At least that was the story we told. In truth, I can't remember how we escaped.

That's because you didn't, you moron. Now wake up. I'm ready to play.

"Jesse, please." I grab his hand. "Your finger."

Leave the baggage.

"No," I say, backing one hand away from the water's edge.

You can't save him if you stay there! Rachel howls. *And I can't hurt them unless you're here. Come on!*

"Jesse!"

Come on!

"Go," he says, almost as if he can hear Rachel too.

"No, I—"

Now!

"Go!" He lifts his hand just enough to grab my shoulder and push me toward the pool. It wouldn't have been enough to force me in if I hadn't let it. But I do. If I lie down and go to sleep beside him, I don't know if I'll remember what I need to remember when I wake up. I have a feeling this isn't the first time we've made the long crawl across the concrete, and I have to know if Rachel's telling the truth. What if Jesse really does need saving?

I hit the water face-first, but there's no splash, just the feel of something slippery oozing free of its confines—an egg falling free from the shell—and my eyes open somewhere else.

The new world is impossibly bright, but I don't dare blink for more than a second. I can feel hands tugging at the backs of my eyes, trying to pull me back under. They want me to give in and let them take me, but I won't go. I know what's real now. The scratchy sheets tucked tight around my legs, the needle in my arm, the feeling that my body has gone unused and I'm hollow inside—this is what's real. Terrifyingly real.

Finally. Do you have any idea how boring it is here?

I try to turn toward Rachel's voice, but can only move my head a few inches. I'm so stiff. How long have I been like this? What's happening? Am I at a hospital? Were we taken here after the crash? Have I been—

Relax, loser. The more excited you get, the more sleepy juice goes into your arm.

I blink again and the edges of Rachel's silhouette come into focus. She's sitting next to me on the bedside table, her feet swinging. I can see the motion, but it takes a few more minutes to pick out the details of her shoes and dress. Finally, her blurred mouth swims into focus beneath her blue eyes

Those meds are bad news. Want me to pull out your IV? She reaches for my arm, but I stop her with a grunt.

No. What's going on? Where am I? What are they treating me for?

They're not treating you for anything. She rolls her eyes, but pulls her hand away. *You're in the bad place with the*

others. You're a little guinea pig and so is he. She points to the bed on the far side of the room where a still form lies hooked to as many monitors as I am.

Jesse. He's thinner than I could have imagined him, pale and wasted with blue veins standing out against his closed lids. If it weren't for the slight rise and fall of his chest, I'd think he was dead.

Why? What is—

They're going to open you up soon. You have to get out of here. If they put that thing in your head we'll both have to play by their rules. Rachel jumps off the table, her shoes clicking lightly on the tile. *And they're even more boring than you are.*

Who's boring?

The men and the women in the pretty white coats. They're the ones in charge of the project.

The Vision Project. Isn't that what Penny said it was called? Penny…

Where's my stepmom? I ask. *Is Penny here, too?*

Penny's dead.

I shake my head. It's easier this time. *No. I've seen her. She was in the place where Jesse and I—*

Rachel snorts. *That's not your place. It's their place. They made that place to keep you asleep and you and doofus made Penny because you feel soooo guilty.* She flips her hair and winks at me over her shoulder. *And you should. It's your fault she's dead.*

Penny's dead. Of course she is. Didn't I know that, someplace deep inside? Isn't that why I didn't question

Rachel when she said that there are people here who needed to be hurt?

I reach up with one trembling hand and peel off the sensors taped to my chest. "That place…sucked." My voice is gravelly and dry, but I can speak. Good. I want the people Rachel and I hurt to know exactly why they're hurting.

Duh. I told you, they're stupid and boring. Rachel reaches for my IV. This time I let her, watching as she removes the tape and slides the needle free with expert fingers. *If they'd really wanted to keep you two asleep, they should have given you a room alone together instead of a stupid pool with monkeys.*

Smart girl, a deep voice says. My head turns in Jesse's direction. His eyes are open and I know the voice in my mind was his.

Can you hear me too? I ask, and I'm rewarded with a small nod. He reaches for the sensors on his own chest and I practically fall out of the bed in my rush to get to him. Thankfully my legs are sturdier than I expected. After a few wobbly moments, I'm steady on my feet and my hands barely tremble as I disconnect his tubes and wires.

When he's free, I help him sit before giving in to the urge to throw my arms around his neck and hug him again in a place that feels real. "I love you. I'm so glad—"

Ew. I can see your pruny white butt, Rachel says. *You realize those gowns don't have backs, right?*

I step away from Jesse with a blush and reach for the back of my gown. He lifts an eyebrow. "She's a real sweetheart, isn't she?" His voice is as scratchy as mine, but he sounds stronger than he looks.

"You can really hear her?"

"I can hear her." He looks over my shoulder. "And I can *see* her."

"What?" I follow his gaze. It's impossible, but he's looking right at where Rachel is perched on the edge of my bed. "But how—"

Can you two stop talking? I'm ready to kill people, Rachel whines, snatching my discarded IV and stabbing it into the bed beneath her.

"No killing," I say, then hurry on before her pout can turn to protest. "But anything else is fine. Just get us through the hospital to a car."

That's it? I can just…go crazy? Totally crazy?

"You can go nuts."

Rachel squeals and jumps off the bed as Jesse swings his legs around and eases onto his feet. "Nuts sound good," he says. "Underwear sounds even better."

"Rachel!" I hiss. She stops at the door and turns back to me. "Bonus points if you can take me and Jesse by a place where we can get food and clothes on the way out."

What kind of bonus points? She sounds suspicious.

I look up at Jesse, at the scar tissue that's kept new hair from growing on one side of his head, and find inspiration. "I'll let you see if you can breathe fire."

She laughs. *Of course I can. I can do anything you imagine I can do.* She takes a breath and aims at the bed I've just crawled out of. Fire explodes from her bloody mouth, a white-orange burst of flame that ignites the sheets in seconds. The pillow goes up next. She turns back to me with her hands propped smugly on her hips. *Now let's go wreak some havoc!*

Rachel dances out the door, but Jesse and I stand where we are, watching the bed burn. After a moment he takes my hand and we follow her into the hall.

Outside, people are already screaming.

About the Author

Anya Parrish was born in Louisiana, grew up in Arkansas, went to school in New York, and found herself in California. She lives in Sonoma County with her family. *Damage* is her first novel. Visit her at anyaparrish.com.